ALSO BY RANDY RUSSELL

Caught Looking

Blind Spot

Hot Wire

DOLL EYES

DOLL EYES

A Rooster Franklin Mystery

Randy Russell

A PERFECT CRIME BOOK

DOUBLEDAY

NEW YORK   LONDON   TORONTO   SYDNEY   AUCKLAND

A PERFECT CRIME BOOK
PUBLISHED BY DOUBLEDAY
a division of Bantam Doubleday Dell Publishing Group, Inc.
666 Fifth Avenue, New York, New York 10103

DOUBLEDAY is a trademark of Doubleday,
a division of Bantam Doubleday Dell
Publishing Group, Inc.

Book design by Tasha Hall

Library of Congress Cataloging-in-Publication Data

Russell, Randy.
Doll eyes : a Rooster Franklin mystery / by Randy Russell.
p.   cm.
"A Perfect Crime book."
I. Title.
PS3568.U7695D65   1992
813'.54—dc20   92-8958
                                                   CIP

ISBN 0-385-42382-9
Copyright © 1992 by Randy Russell
Printed in the United States of America
September 1992

1   3   5   7   9   10   8   6   4   2

First Edition in the United States of America

*For the original members of
the After Hours Club—both
in front of and behind bars.*

The mind has a thousand eyes,
And the heart but one.

—FRANCIS WILLIAM BOURDILLON

DOLL EYES

Prologue

Marc Morelli had plans. He wasn't going to pan for gold when he got out. Or write a novel or join a band. His first day out of the federal pen at Leavenworth, Morelli was going to take back what was left of his family business in Kansas City. His family business was crime.

He'd reestablish control on the Kansas side, collecting those associates who'd remained loyal into a cohesive and potent organization, disposing of those who'd decided to free-lance while Morelli was in The House. It wouldn't take long. Morelli knew how to go about such things. Then he'd locate the person who put him here.

Morelli thought he might thank Rooster Franklin for taking care of the old man. His grandfather's death had placed Marc in command of the KCK syndicate. But before he thanked Rooster Franklin, Morelli plotted breaking both the bastard's kneecaps.

"It's like this," Morelli told his cellmate. "You take some of the powder out. You know, lighten the load a little. Then you cut a deep cross in the lead to split the bullet into four parts when it fires. You can do it with a butter knife. Yeah, I like that. A butter knife. I'll turn his asshole into duck butter. What you think?"

"You gonna shove that gun up his colon?"

"Colon? Where'd you get a word like that? But you're right. Maybe I'll have to file off the sight. I'll get it up there. You want to watch? Hey, when do you get out anyway?"

"I don't, remember? I don't."

"Maybe I'll practice on your ass then," Morelli offered. "You know, get it just right."

Then he'd put a couple rounds in Rooster's face. In the middle of his face. Morelli wanted the bullets to split Rooster's upper lip, take out the top teeth right in the middle of his face. After that, he'd show Rooster Franklin some gratitude for having taken care of the old man.

Yeah, he'd be, what you call it, demonstrative. Finding Rooster would be a breeze. Morelli would coerce his sister, the little shit, into helping. Rosalinda could put her finger on Franklin as easy as most people fart after eating burritos.

Marc Morelli had plans for Rooster. He was going to get that boy.

One

No matter how far I went, no matter how long I was gone, I never got clean away from her.

I shouldn't have taken a plane to Kansas City. I was going to get there just the same. But I was in a hurry. My mother called it "having a feather in your shorts." I supposed it was something heavier than a feather that was jerking my life around.

The house on Fairmount Street looked as much like home as any other place I'd ever stayed. I climbed out of the taxi with my duffel bag, thinking I should have driven the van to Kansas City. Just in case she didn't want me back again.

There's one woman in every man's life. Rosalinda was mine. My mother would have laughed at this one-woman crap. But she wasn't a man. Men know the truth: one woman whose scent you recall in the heat of every battle, whose laughter you hear when your intestines hit the emergency room floor, whose smile you see any time you close your eyes. Whose desperate, red-faced, gasping clench you remember when other women come under you.

You can't even think her name without getting a feather in your shorts.

It had been two years since we lived together. When I run from a woman, I run fast, hard, and long. Guess I come back in the same fashion.

It didn't matter if she didn't want to see me. I'd make her want me again. Whatever was wrong, I'd fix. Maybe my mother didn't hold with this one-woman stuff. But, let me tell you, in every woman's life there's only one man. I'm Rosalinda's.

I'm Alton Benjamin Franklin. A bigger idiot you've never met. But I was in love. Hard in love. Close up or faraway forever, being in love ruins a good intellect. It's also been known to cost a man a few good bones, organs by which he needs to breathe.

There's a saying where I come from. I come from the hard-rock mining towns of northeastern Oklahoma: Picher, Cardin, Alkali, and Rust. The saying is *She isn't worth a lung.*

You could be talking about a horse who came in last. Or about a woman who did you wrong. It's true. She wasn't worth a lung. Rosalinda was worth two. She was the reason I breathed. You lie down on your back and take a breath, slowly, you'll feel her name pass over your tongue.

"Welcome home," I said out loud to the September morning. There were birds, actually singing, in the sunlit tree in Rosalinda's front yard. Nothing they could do would make me dislike them.

The tree was an Eastern redbud. Thick now with heart-shaped leaves and slender pods at the end of summer, it stood a full forty feet. Rosalinda had first seen the tree in spring, covered with blossoms turned from white to dark pink by the blood of Judas, who'd hanged himself from the branches of a forebear of this tree.

The tree was part of the reason Rosalinda had bought the small, two-story clapboard, the house where I once thought I might live forever and now wasn't so sure I wouldn't. The road gets old no matter how many horses you nail at the wire. I'd hit a Pick-Six. I had money and life to burn. Rosalinda was where I knew to find my spark. What did a lousy couple of years have to do with anything?

I rocked lazily in the wooden swing on Rosalinda's front porch. It would be a long wait. I remembered a time Rosalinda and I had made love on the swing. We'd both been drinking, as your attorney is apt to say when your crime finally comes to court. The judge, in turn, asks how many drinks. I don't know a person in the whole damn world who counts.

We made love in the swing at night at the end of summer. We made love with most of our clothes on, rocking, swinging, tipping forward and back. We'd come home from somewhere late and we couldn't wait until we were inside the house. This was my memory of Fairmount Street.

My flight got in a bit after ten o'clock. I was at the house on Fairmount Street because I didn't want to bother her at work. I wanted to be a surprise she came home to.

I could show up at the art gallery unannounced, but that risked being treated like a customer by the one woman of my entire life. I wasn't buying, thank you. I'd already bought. I used the time to check for signs another man might be hanging around. One of those possibilities I could easily take care of. I peeked in through the first-story windows.

You bet the farm or the bet isn't worth making. Coming back to Kansas City was my way of betting the farm. Not to mention those vital organs we already talked about.

I practiced the names of the potted cactuses lined along the south railing of the porch. The stubby, thorny plants had survived my absence, but they should have grown more in the time I'd been away. I blamed it on George Bush being in the White House.

A stoic friend caught my attention. It was a six-foot wooden sculpture tucked into the far corner of the porch. It was obviously one of Rosalinda's works. I tried to come up with a name for it. The sculpture was brightly painted and might have been either an American Indian or a horse standing on its rear legs. It might have been me.

Eventually, I rocked myself silly in that swing. I could wait no longer. I found the key where I knew it would be, on the hook behind the concrete step to the porch. I unlocked the front door.

Setting my bag inside, I noticed instantly that Rosalinda had remodeled. The curtains were different. The furniture was new and the walls were beige instead of white. These changes ruined the picture I carried in my mind of what home was supposed to look like. So did the mess.

Half-empty glasses, beer bottles, overflowing ashtrays, and stained paper plates were strategically placed about the room. The remnants of a cheese-ball buffet decorated the dining room table. Liquor and soda bottles, some uncapped, lined the matching bleached-oak sideboard.

Still, the detritus of a party the night before (one hoped) bothered me much less than the more substantive changes. I hated the new curtains. I hated the furniture. Come winter, I told myself, it would look more like home again. Rosalinda would move the cactus indoors.

I used the downstairs bathroom. A shave would wait, I decided. Rosalinda enjoyed watching me shave. It was a time for her to talk and for me to listen. It was a time I looked forward to. I'd be wearing only my jockey shorts and tattoo. Rosalinda would be drawing a bath. Watching her in the mirror, instead of paying attention to what I was doing, I'd cut myself. It would sting sharply and I'd be in love for the first time all over again.

The house on Fairmount was a few blocks inside the state line, between the brass and glass of the Country Club Plaza to the south and the cluster of tourist restaurants, faddish bars, antique shops, and art galleries of Westport to the north. I hiked to Forty-third Street. At the brick bank on the Kansas side of State Line Road, I changed a handful of traveler's checks into a personal checking account, using Rosalinda's house for my address. The brief ceremony established myself not only as a citizen of the city but as a proper resident of Rosalinda's future life.

It wasn't marriage, but it felt like it. Our vows were witnessed on my signature card. A bank lobby was close enough to being a chapel for me. If only my bride had been there. I kissed the bank good-bye and crossed back into Missouri.

Jack's Tavern, the sole remaining neighborhood bar on Forty-third, was dark. As it should be. Kansas City is a community with two rivers, the one through hell and the other through Missouri. You can sit in Jack's Tavern and spit in Kansas. It sizzles. The debate in Jack's is whether we prefer to find beyond death hell or Kansas City, Missouri. It's a bar with a back door.

A shot of Johnnie Walker Red with a draft back was my sure cure for jet lag. I stood at the bar, slugged back the shot, and was sipping a Boulevard draw by the time my vision adjusted to the dark-moon atmosphere of Jack's single long and narrow room. Two people I recognized sat in a back booth, reading different sections of the same newspaper in the glow of a ten-watt beer sign.

I approached Ray Sargent, Jr., and Angelo Metoyer, founding members of the After Hours Club. Standing at the edge of their booth, I waited for either to look up from the Kansas City *Star*.

"Holy shit," Ray finally exclaimed. "It's Rooster." His open-mouth expression said he might have just seen Elvis shopping nude at the local 7-Eleven.

"Hey, pal," Metro said coolly, as if he and I had merely been keeping an appointment. Metro offered a sincere, wide smile and I felt instantly as if I'd never left town.

Metro, who worked in the public relations office at the University of Kansas Medical Center, was Creole. He took pains to accept his friends as members of his family. His job had long ago become a cover for his true occupation, booking wagers on all major sporting events, and many minor ones, for the employees at the medical center and for anyone else in midtown who knew his phone number.

Ray appeared taller than his six-foot height because he was thin from top to bottom. He wrote weekly travel articles for a Los Angeles syndication and had never been to L.A. In fact, Ray traveled very little, preferring to fill his column with obscure facts about unusual locations rather than with travel anecdotes and hotel accommodations.

Ray also dabbled in private investigations. Many in town believed he relied on the high-tech resources of his father's well-established security corporation. Truth was you couldn't be sure whether he and his father were on talking terms. Ray Sargent, Jr. was resourceful and self-reliant in his own right.

"Where'd you go this week?" I asked, sliding into the booth next to Ray, comfortable among friends.

"Cuba," Ray said. "Where you've been is the question."

"He's not kidding," Metro warned. "The guy wrote this column on the resorts in Cuba even though Americans can't go there."

"People should know what they're missing," Ray argued.

"How's business?" I asked quickly, before Ray could ask me again what I'd been up to since last having a drink with the After Hours Club.

"Added sixteen papers in the last six months. And Metro here has had to hire help."

It was bad news for Metro. The inevitable had happened.

There was an organization in town that made it a practice to offer free-lance bookies with growing businesses their own collection and payoff services. A working bookmaker then had the choice, either go out of business or let the organization move in. In some cities, they're called the Mafia.

"I may get out altogether," Metro said under his breath. Nobody believed him. "Those damn Royals," Metro added hastily. "I tell you, they don't beat Milwaukee tonight they're out of it. You can write off the AL West."

"Oakland's already clinched the division," I said.

"Yeah," Metro drawled. "I'm talking about writing off next year, too."

"So what are you up to these days?" Ray asked.

"Looking for Rosalinda." I told the truth.

By mentioning her name, I killed the conversation. They both glanced away. It didn't make sense. Ray and Metro were friends of hers as much as they were friends of mine. Rosalinda had been a regular member of the After Hours Club, a loose affiliation of people who got along with each other and had nothing more in common than that. And the fact we needed to drink with someone besides ourselves occasionally.

Different people rotated through the After Hours Club, but when you needed a friend, someone nonjudgmental, you knew where to look. The club was an AA group waiting to happen. And we just happened to meet in bars. Sometimes we stayed till closing.

"Check this out," Ray finally said, dodging the subject of Rosalinda. He handed a folded section of the newspaper to me as a diversion. The story was about a CIA employee who bought a sheet of one-dollar "candlestick inverts" at the post office that had later been sold for a tidy profit by a group of his colleagues. The candle flame, a separate color from the rest of the postage stamp, had been mistakenly printed upside down.

"Can you believe it?" Ray wanted to know. "A new stamp worth a hundred grand and the CIA comes up with it?"

I scanned the article without comment, struggling to quiet the uneasiness that had arisen at the mention of Rosalinda.

"You get that bus line started yet?" I asked Ray, putting aside the paper.

He grinned. A couple years back, when tourist trolleys were introduced to take visitors from the Country Club Plaza to Crown Center and back, Ray came up with the idea of offering glass-bottom bus tours of Kansas City.

"It would work," Ray said. "You have any idea what you can see on the streets of this city?"

"Potholes and condoms," Metro said. "Coke vials and spent cartridges."

"You haven't come up with someone to paint the fish, buried treasure, and human skeletons along the route yet?" I asked.

"No," Ray confessed with regret. "And I haven't talked anyone into painting the striptease you suggested either."

"You mean the dancer taking off her clothes in synchronization with the speed of the bus?" I teased.

"Use pros," Metro chimed in. "Hell, they know enough to keep their heads down. You ever see how much room there is under a bus? Who needs art when you can have the real thing?"

"Soon to be an Olympic event," I suggested.

"The guy's nuts, Rooster. I meet him for an early lunch, on a Monday; mind you, a Monday after he's taken all my spare money on the NFL games. And besides asking me if I want to lay it all off on tonight's game, he makes fun of my plans."

"On a Monday," I repeated solemnly, sadly shaking my head in Metro's wide-eyed direction.

"He treats me like I'm ethnic, Rooster," Metro said, taking his turn to complain.

"You are ethnic," Ray reminded him.

"That's not the point. You sit there thinking I dance."

"You do dance."

"That's not the point."

People who didn't know better would have thought they were arguing. The lunchtime waitress appeared, sat down a fresh pitcher of Boulevard, and slipped into the seat next to Metro.

"Why aren't you at work?" she asked him, then noticed who was sitting across from her. "Rooster?" she said. "Rooster, is that you?"

"In the flesh," Ray replied for me.

Beth Rogers smiled broadly. She kicked at me under the table.

"I don't believe this," she said. "You son of a bitch, stand up and let me look at you."

I obliged and Beth stood with me to share a hug. Beth was small and as cute as one of those stuffed animals you can win at carnivals. She smelled the same, I noticed, pleased to be discovering that so few things had changed.

"You look good as a blonde," I said. Well, some things change. She may have had different hair color, but she was the same person. I guessed we all were.

"You back for awhile?" Beth asked as we sat back down.

"I believe I am," I said. "But that depends on Rosalinda."

Beth's eyes stopped smiling. She glanced awkwardly away and the four of us were treated to a chilling silence. Ray, Metro, and Beth tried not to look at me, tried not to look at each other.

"I may as well tell you," I said a bit angrily. "I mean to marry the girl."

Two

The lunch crowd had come and gone. I hadn't eaten.

Three or four people sat at the bar in Jack's, watching television and talking quietly when they spoke at all. A country song ended on the jukebox and none came on to follow it. Ray had already left.

"Got to check in at the office," Metro said. "Might be a couple calls. I tell you what, pick a number for the Chiefs and I'll choose over or under. Make it wins."

I was ready for this. I'd been following the Kansas City teams since my departure. A bet on the Chiefs meant I officially lived in town again. The Chiefs were two wins, one loss thus far. The team looked ready to gel.

"Twelve," I said. "Twelve wins."

"Less," Metro said swiftly. "You always were a dreamer, Rooster."

The bet was sixty-nine beers, the usual among the members of the After Hours Club. What it came down to, since everybody owed everybody sixty-nine beers, was that whoever had money bought the rounds. Twelve wins would put the Chiefs in the playoffs with home-field advantage.

Metro leaned forward before leaving and said in a hushed voice, "Marc Morelli was let out. Word is he wants to chew you a new asshole."

I nodded. Metro stood and pointed at me in parting. "Keep trim," he said.

It meant I was supposed to keep my eyes and ears open, I was supposed to stay alert. Nothing new in Metro saying good-bye this way. But it sounded more like a sincere warning than a casual parting.

I moved to the booth nearest the front door. Beth brought coffee around, then came back over with a large plate of french fries, a squirt bottle of ketchup, and two forks.

"You need a lift somewhere?" she asked. "It's okay if I take a break about this time."

Being home was the only lift I needed. She sat across from me and ate in silence until most of the fries were gone.

"You're just like Mike," she said, raising her green eyes to mine, switching moods. She jabbed the empty air between us with her fork. "You all think you're cowboys or something. I was eighteen and pregnant and I was stupid enough to cosign for twenty-four payments on a new Harley. The bastard made the first one and was gone."

"For good," I said, stressing it. Beth was lucky to have learned this lesson while she was young. When you're older, the bastards really take you to the cleaners. I tried to think of a way to express this without insulting her or giving her the impression I was unsympathetic. I came up empty.

"What gets me is I bought the damn cycle he rode out on. That's the law when you cosign. They can go after both or either of you and for some dumb-ass reason I wanted to stay in town."

"How's your kid?" I managed to ask.

"Okay. Really, you know, Mom helps out while I'm at work and I'm taking upper-level day classes now at UMKC."

"Painting?"

"I figured you'd get around to that. Rooster, the world

has changed since we were kids. My major's electrical design."

"Computers or toasters?" I tried. Beth sounded quite certain of the world for someone who wasn't thirty yet. Still, I was pleased she had included me in her own age group. That will put a feather in your shorts every time.

"It's a tad more technical than that. Besides, I wasn't that good. I mean, I never really had the drive to paint. It was just something I could do."

"I always liked your paintings, Beth. Remember the group show at Rosalinda's gallery? Yours was about the only stuff that sold."

"That's because I painted hokey stuff, Rooster. People buy hokey stuff. On top of which, my mother bought three of the damn things herself."

Beth wiped the plate with the last french fry. There were several hours to kill before Rosalinda came home from work. But I couldn't just sit there and eat clock. I brought up what mattered most to me.

"Tell me about Rosalinda," I said.

Beth attempted a smile. "That's why I'm here," she said without animosity, "to talk to men about other women." She sighed. "Well, Rooster, she's uptown is the best way to put it."

"Making money?"

"Worse. She reopened the gallery at a corner location in Westport. It's called Inside Moves and she's gone straight establishment. I can't blame her, really. The alternative gallery was a good idea and I know she loved doing it. But, well, things change. She's making money and her gallery's like all the rest. Boring."

It didn't sound like Rosalinda at all.

"Inside Moves, as you might guess from the name, caters to interior decorators, people who buy signed and numbered prints not only as an investment but to match the sofa. The sculpture, Rooster, is all bronze and fits snugly on a coffee table or mantel. It's nothing like the pieces she used to do."

I rudely thought of myself as one of the pieces she used to do.

"Oh, and she has a partner, Rooster. Some guy from back East, D.C. or something like that. He's brought in all these expensive art objects. Antique porcelains. Staffordshire."

"Yeah, but—"

"She has nothing to do with young artists anymore. She doesn't even show her own pieces. She gave them away to friends when she moved into the new place."

"Yeah, but how's she doing?" I asked, undaunted, trying to keep a sense of humor, trying to mask my deeper feelings, my longing.

"Fine, just fine. Of course, nobody I know has seen much of her lately. I'm telling you, Rooster, she's in tight with the Mission crowd. You could probably find her at the country club right now if they're still serving lunch."

"What the hell, Beth. Everybody needs to make a buck once in a while. You wouldn't know her partner's name?"

"Warman," Beth said after a pause. There was a fleeting apprehension in Beth's eyes when she answered the simple question. "Let me tell you about women, Rooster. We've got doll eyes, you know what I'm saying? The kind that close when you lay the doll down on its back. They open again when you stand the doll up."

I pictured it. But Beth could read my expression. I didn't know what she was getting at.

"A woman lays down with a guy, her eyes close. Just like that. She no longer sees anything. She can't see any fault in the guy she's with. A girl goes to bed with a normal guy and wakes up seeing hearts and flowers."

"Come on, Beth. You know better than that."

"Maybe not the first time. Maybe not every guy. But sooner or later, you lay a girl down and her eyes snap closed.

Doll eyes, Rooster. Next thing you know she's out shopping for a Harley."

I'd had just enough beer to enjoy walking. I got into it. It felt like an adventure. Some people count cadence as they walk, others recite poetry or sing songs to themselves. I can't tell you how happy I was strolling back to Rosalinda's place except to say I kept giggling. A grown man with the giggles on the streets of midtown is apt to be arrested.

The afternoon sun was warm and backyard dogs lazily soaked up the end of summer. I hoped to get in a couple hours sleep in my new time zone before Rosalinda came home from work.

I'd left the door unlocked, which wasn't like me. Not that I have much faith in locks, but they do serve to keep the neighborhood grade-schoolers from going through your sock drawers. Sometimes.

Once inside the house, I couldn't sit still, let alone lie down. I resisted the urge to go through her things, to pick up and study a few details of what her life had been the past two years. Rosalinda may have been putting on the Ritz in Westport, but she certainly wasn't living like royalty at home. I also resisted the urge to pick up the place.

I'd eaten few of Beth's french fries and suddenly I was hungry. Checking the refrigerator, I found it to be barren of anything I would eat. Then I had a wonderful idea. I'd fix supper for the two of us.

This meant I had to get back out there in all that Kansas City sunshine and promenade to the grocery store. Maybe I'd see Mickey Mantle at the meat counter, I thought. Maybe he'd shake my hand. I started giggling again. It was that kind of day.

A green Ford sedan with Kansas plates was parked down the block on Fairmount. It looked like a car I'd seen in the rear parking lot of Jack's. No one was in the car so I shrugged it off. I was in too good of a mood to notice holes in that sunlight.

Like a cave man, we'd eat what I could carry. You can't live in the Midwest without knowing how to charcoal steaks. They teach it in Sunday school when you're three. I picked up a hibachi-size grill pan and rack, a sack of charcoal, lighter, and two sixteen-ounce rib-eyes. For reasons someone will have to explain to me someday, they always sell corn on the cob in packages of three.

I'd have to run with my day's kill to keep the ice cream from melting. I bought two bottles of wine. "Yabba dabba-do," I said to the wooden sculpture on the porch as I set down my sacks. Rosalinda would change her name to Wilma, I thought. We'd get married and have a dog shaped like a dinosaur. Who needs salad when you're celebrating your new life as a happily married man?

I guess you could say I'd made up my mind.

I stored the grub. It was too early to start the coals. I wandered around, ending up in the backyard. There was room for a big dog here. We could build on a little deck. Flowers would bloom in neat clumps along the fence. I'd get one of those fancy gas grills on our first anniversary.

I told myself the truth: There wasn't a better place in the world than Rosalinda's house on Fairmount Street from which to order a five-year subscription to the *Daily Racing Form*. I'd have my own reading lamp and three colors of pens.

Then I decided there was time to wash and dry the sheets. Rosalinda never made her bed. I'd strip it, get it going in the basement, and maybe have time for a short nap. The chair I used to sit in was missing.

It had been a wingback chair reupholstered in a loud Hawaiian print. Rosalinda and I had made love in the chair, standing up. We bounced up and down in each other's arms on the seat cushion. When we collapsed into the chair, it fell over backwards and we continued making love on the floor. I was fond of that chair. Maybe she'd stored it in the basement, I thought, climbing the stairs to the bedroom.

The larger upstairs room was Rosalinda's studio. I left that door unopened.

The mess in Rosalinda's bedroom was far worse than anything downstairs. The room smelled like old piss. When I saw her I stood frozen in the doorway of the bedroom for what seemed like hours without taking a breath.

Her king-size waterbed had been replaced with a four-poster. She was tied face down by ankle and wrist to each of the posts. And there was blood. Plenty of blood. Too much blood. Her skin was the wrong color.

I was much too calm for the way I felt. My pounding heart wanted out of my chest. My stomach ached. You could hear my pain. It sounded like a freight train exploding. It sounded like bells. She was dead.

And I felt worse than dead. Someone was pounding on the front door. You can bet it wasn't me who called the cops.

Three

I was brought from the holding cell to the third floor of the municipal building, this time to Lieutenant Warren Felker's office. We'd met before. It was the fourth time I'd tell the homicide detective my story. Felker sat at a small metal desk in a room with no windows. He didn't stand up when I was ushered in.

"Choose a chair," he said without looking at me.

The room was done up in four wooden chairs and sixteen file cabinets. A picture of Felker's wife and three little lieutenants was propped atop the metal desk otherwise covered with folders, loose papers, and a single coffee mug.

"What can I tell you?" Felker asked the air with an uplifting of both hands, palms empty. "Your story checks out. Three neighbors saw you get out of the cab. One got the cab number."

"That would be Mrs. Ross," I said.

"Whatever," he said, dismissing my interruption. "Cabby remembers picking you up. Your airplane ticket was in your bag. Your seat was occupied on the flight by someone wearing the same clothes and who looked a lot like you. They have a video of each passenger disembarking at KCI. Did you know that?''

I did now.

Felker's swept-back blond hair was graying. His full mustache drooped over the corners of his mouth. His brown suit was only slightly less wrinkled than the shirt and pants I wore. Felker's tie, I noted, was navy blue with tiny red specks. The pin dots were so small the tie appeared purple upon first glance. It was the color the sky looked when you sprayed it with blood.

Felker looked as tired as I felt. There was only one bench in the holding cell, and four other unhappy citizens there had kept me from stretching out. The floor was littered with cigarette butts. I'd paced, avoiding conversation, recalling with a shudder every third step that awful moment, those few tremulous seconds when I'd believed it was Rosalinda's body stretched out naked and dead on the four-poster.

The dead woman wasn't her. The two-story on Fairmount, I'd later learn, wasn't any longer Rosalinda's house.

"We also talked to the girl in Seattle, Franklin, and she backs you up. Know what's next?''

"I can't leave town."

"Right you are. And, while we appreciate your apparent cooperation, I have to tell you it's time you get a lawyer. The individual who discovers and reports a murder is in all cases a suspect."

I started to speak, but Felker waved me off.

"That's right," he said. "You claim you didn't make that call. Well, whoever did said he was you." Felker paused. "I'm going to think about that," he concluded.

So was I.

"Speaking of which, we received a phone call, Franklin. You have a friend in the right place, it seems. I want you to know, however, friends won't do you a damn bit of good if you try to run out on me."

He let it sink in.

"I'm not horse-assing around, Rooster. I have a bench warrant for your arrest."

It was well after midnight and I was accustomed now to waiting for Felker's punch lines.

"Trespassing," he said. "Unlawful entry. All it takes is my rubber stamp and you're a wanted man. Trespassing with intent *and* suspicion of murder, of course. If that gets tiring, I can always hold you on car theft, don't you think?"

He had me there. Lieutenant Felker and I had met before.

"Twenty-five cars a day are stolen in this little city. I hold you for one one day, another the next. I could hold you for years on auto theft, Franklin. You understand that? Forty-eight hours and then I have another fifty thefts to choose from."

There was a flaw in his plan, but I wasn't about to point it out to him. He had to let me out for an hour or so once in a while so I'd have opportunity.

"Am I free to go?" I had no idea who might have called Felker to get me released tonight instead of tomorrow.

"Your bag's downstairs at the desk. Though I'm certain we'll be talking again, if you remember anything you haven't told us, feel free to call. We're running the usual tests."

They'd taken samples from my person, including sweat, saliva, semen, and scrapings from under my fingernails. I'd also been instructed to bite a small block of paraffin to record the impression of my teeth. Hairs had been plucked from my head, chest, underarms, legs, and genitals.

Felker was making a big mistake, though, if he were approaching the murder as a sex crime. The girl had been shot in the head execution-style. If she'd been molested, it had occurred as a cover-up.

"Who was she?" I asked, standing up from the hard wooden chair, wondering if I could really leave.

"Read about it in the papers. I'm not the public information officer."

Right.

"One more thing," Felker said as my hand reached for the door. I turned to face him.

The lieutenant held out an envelope for me. "The lady," he said, "wanted you to have this."

"Rosalinda?"

"Whoever." Felker shrugged. The envelope wasn't sealed. On police stationery, a local phone number had been scrawled in what I took to be the lieutenant's hand. There was nothing more.

Downstairs, I asked if a ride could be provided.

"Temporary blackout," the sergeant told me. "No patrols available for dispatch."

That was comforting to know. I wondered if I could get them to call me the next time it happened. There was a jewelry store on Forty-third I wouldn't mind visiting after hours when there was another temporary blackout.

I stepped outside into the cool morning, facing a series of at least a hundred concrete steps to the street. I paused to survey the night sky. There were a few scattered clouds and a fine, fattening moon. Once I reached the sidewalk, I turned to carry my duffel bag to the corner where, I hoped, a cab would be waiting at the stand. I needn't have bothered.

A gold Mercedes 450SL convertible, facing the wrong direction, backed along the curb to catch up to me. The driver was no one I recognized. A well-groomed face beamed at me with smiling but serious intent.

"Need a lift?" the stranger called over the irritating whine of a Mercedes moving in reverse. I stopped walking. "Rosalinda sent me."

Without waiting for my reply, the driver—tall and clean-cut—threw it in park and hopped out of the convertible. He offered to take my duffel bag. "We'll need to put that in the boot," he said.

I carried the bag around the back of the car and waited for my gracious host to open the trunk. Once he slammed down the lid, he turned and offered a hand along with a we're-in-business-now grin.

"Joseph Warman," he said, still smiling with an air of understood complicity. His watch was a gold Gucci that matched his tan, which in turn matched the color of his Mercedes, all of which seemed personally designed to make his perfectly shaped teeth appear whiter, especially at night. His upper lip was decorated with a tightly trimmed mustache that, unlike Felker's droopy variety, failed to brush the edge of his lip.

"Call me Joe," he suggested.

It seemed obvious the man knew who I was. I accepted the handshake.

"How is she?" I asked, releasing Mr. Tan's manicured grip.

"Oh, she's holding up. A bit shaken, naturally. But she'll be fine. Just fine. Hop on in. A real trooper, Rosalinda."

Joseph Warman slithered back into the driver's seat as I squeezed carefully in the passenger seat. Leather buckets.

"Well, now, where are you headed?" Warman asked nonchalantly as the Mercedes popped away from the curb with a bark of rubber burning on the pavement. Warman belatedly hooked his seat belt and shoulder harness.

"Your place?" I finally said as Warman brought the convertible to a quick fake stop to turn from Eleventh Street onto Main heading south. The Mercedes lurched forward and ran the light at Twelfth. Someone must have told Warman about the temporary blackout of available patrol units.

I studied the faceted gold ring on Warman's left hand. It glinted under the streetlights as he handled the steering wheel. The wind in my face was extremely cold, as if autumn had arrived a month early.

"I'm afraid that would be a wee awkward tonight," Warman was saying in reply to my suggestion I camp out at his place. If you didn't know better you'd have thought Warman had actually considered the possibility and was truly troubled by not being able to offer me the hospitality of his abode. I knew better.

I feared worse.

"You're married?" I asked loudly. "You and Rosalinda are . . ."

Warman grinned as if he were in on a joke.

"That's right," he said. "I thought you knew. Quite an escapade you had with her family a few years back, wasn't it? Well, that's all over now. The past, you know what I'm saying?"

"The Best Western on Rainbow will do just fine," I said.

"That's in Kansas, isn't it?"

"Try Thirty-ninth Street west," I offered. Try driving this gold buggy straight to hell, Joe Warman. The past? The past hadn't even started to begin yet. Rosalinda wasn't my past, pal. She was my future and I was here to see to it.

As we drove from under the Power and Light Building, I noticed the art deco dome of the building was green. It turned different colors periodically. Warman, I decided, had mistaken it for a traffic light.

We finally stopped for a red light at Pershing Road, the massive and historic Union Station on our right. I considered telling Warman about the machine-gun massacre that had taken place in the parking lot of the train station one June day in 1933. I wished he'd been caught in the crossfire.

The massacre was a mob hit on Frank "Jelly" Nash, who wore a red wig at the time of his demise. He was being transported to Leavenworth by federal agents, who'd captured the elusive bank robber in Hot Springs, Arkansas. They rode the Missouri Pacific Flyer from Fort Smith to Kansas City's Union Station.

As Nash was loaded into one of two waiting cars, the group was sprayed with machine-gun fire. I could have told Warman the license plate numbers of the cars: Missouri 39–886 and Nebraska 1–4995. Nash, and just about everybody accompanying him, including three FBI agents, were killed.

The funny thing about the massacre was that a number of otherwise respectable citizens had known about it in advance. A daughter of city manager Henry McElroy had invited her boyfriend, underworld figure Blackie Audett, to view the grisly affair as if it were a movie and they were on a date.

The gangster wearing a red wig was one of those trivial bits of information I found impossible to forget, like making love standing up in a wingback chair of Hawaiian print. Wearing a red wig on your way to prison was asking for it was the only moral I could come up with for the story.

The station, named after the victors of the War Between the States fought by bloody bushwhackers along the border between Missouri and hell, loomed large enough to house a football stadium. The interior of the massive edifice badly needed refurbishing, so much so that the actual train station was now housed inside a two-story geodesic tent erected inside the building.

I thought of the lovers kissing good-bye, of the numberless women waiting for a train to arrive with someone like myself on board, returning home after a two-year absence. The only one waiting for me now was an unknown motel maid who'd bang on the door later that day when I overslept.

We drove by the towering Crown Center, the hotel with a waterfall in the lobby and more than a few hundred pie-shaped rooms. The shops there were little more than tourist traps, much like those you'd find in a Las Vegas casino lobby. Only people from out of town, or out of their minds, shopped at the Crown.

Warman waited in his gold car while I booked a room at the motel across the boulevard from the University of Kansas Medical Center. This was my old neighborhood and the motel was perfectly situated. There was a 7-Eleven less than a block away, a Waid's Restaurant for breakfast, and numerous fast food establishments. It was somewhat comforting to know that Metro's office was just across the street.

Warman opened the passenger door as I came out of the office. My room was around back. Warman drove the two of us to the appropriate slot, killed the lights, and put it in park without turning the engine off. He touched me on the arm to keep me from climbing out just yet.

"We may as well talk here," Warman said.

Lights reflected eerily off the surface of the swimming pool in sporadic waves upon the brick wall of the motel we sat facing.

"The thing is, Franklin, now don't get me wrong, but if you could have mistaken Kathleen for Rosalinda so could somebody else. I don't mind telling you we're a bit worried."

"The idea being?"

"Perhaps the pervert *was* after Rosalinda . . . as a way to, uh, get to *you.*"

"Me?"

"You come into town, the girl's dead."

"The girl was dead *before* I came into town."

"But perhaps someone knew you were heading this way."

"I don't follow you," I said.

"To be candid, Rosalinda tells me you live a rather, uh, underground lifestyle, gambling and such."

"Have you met the bride's family?" I blurted out. Talk about underworld.

"But she has absolutely nothing to do with her brother anymore. They don't speak to each other."

I was tired of this. "Who was she, Warman? The dead girl, who was she?"

"Kathleen?"

The question was obvious.

"It's funny. I started to say nobody. Very rude of me. But I suppose now she is nobody. Never mind that. Kathleen was a friend of Rosalinda's. She was an artist of some promise, Franklin. Rosalinda and I were bringing her along."

"Was she brought there?" I asked, bristling at the thought of Rosalinda and Warman bringing someone along.

"What?"

"Was she killed, then placed in the house?"

"Oh, I see," he said, almost chuckling. "No, it was her house. Kathleen's. Rosalinda had sold it to her. The police didn't tell you?"

"They told me I might be arrested for trespassing."

"You might have used the phone book," Warman said.

"But the cactus?"

"Well, yes, I'm afraid Rosalinda let them go with the house. Kathleen was rather fond of the prickly things."

Not only was he from out of town, I concluded, Warman wasn't trying too awfully hard to assimilate. He leaned across the leather passenger seat and once again offered me his hand. For a moment I was afraid he might actually wink. For a moment I was afraid I might bite off his thumb. There's only so much of the chivalry crap a guy can stomach.

The trunk lid popped up on its own. I walked around, grabbed my bag, and slammed shut the lid.

"By the way," Warman said, in place of backing up over one of my feet, "I'm certain Rosalinda would like to see you before you leave town."

Four

I wasn't leaving town. I was just beginning to like the place.

The plan had been to pop the question, fly back to Seattle with Rosalinda, pick up my van parked at a friend's house not far from Longacres, and take a cross-country honeymoon drive back to Kansas City. Sunday night in the airport at Seattle it had all made perfect sense.

Now my overriding sense was one of exhaustion. I dumped the contents of my duffel bag on one bed, undressed, and lay face down on the other bed. The scrawled phone number haunted my thoughts. What if *he* answered the phone.

I'd assumed Rosalinda would be dating someone, but not someone who mattered to her more than I did. Two years wasn't that long for our lives to have run whatever circles were required to bring the two of us back together again. She'd screwed it up marrying that jerk. But we could fix that.

Rosalinda and I should have been in each other's arms by now.

A dead woman obscenely strapped to a bed wasn't the homecoming I'd anticipated. I stretched out my arms and legs, spreading them like wings, feeling each wrist, each ankle being tied to the bed. I made my body go numb until it felt paralyzed. Until each limb was far too heavy to move even if I'd wanted it to. Dead weight, I thought, is what our bodies are.

Death takes place inside the body somehow. I felt the bullet that had killed Kathleen push back a flap of skin and enter my skull, turning my hair a dark, sticky, sinister color. I felt the helplessness of being left in such a position. I was too frightened to cry.

I rolled suddenly over on my back to break the spell of apprehension and was awash in a wave of loneliness. That's what being dead was, I decided, loneliness. Dying was only fear. You can live with fear.

I was lonely for Rosalinda. She was so damn near. It was cruel being in the same city, our city, and not being able to see her. I finally fell asleep on top of the covers, daunted by the large number of reasons a woman might be murdered.

It was easily noon before I was shaved, showered, and wearing fresh clothes. My mind swam back to yesterday. I remembered the unlocked door at Rosalinda's house. But Kathleen had been dead at least a day before I got there.

Stopping by the motel desk, I booked my room for another night. I ate a large breakfast, spiced by four aspirin, at the Waid's next door. I read the paper. There was the usual number of reports of violence for a given Tuesday. This Tuesday included an item that reported the finding of the body of Kathleen Kelly, thirty-one, in her home on Fairmount Street. The Metropolitan Squad, a cooperative team of detectives from the various municipalities that make up greater Kansas City, would investigate the homicide under the direction of Lieutenant Warren Felker, KCMO Police Department. Funeral services were being arranged by a Moravian mortuary in Winston-Salem. Kathleen was survived by her parents, residents of North Carolina.

Kathleen had lived in Kansas City for just more than five

years, the last four of which were spent as a student at the Art Institute. A late bloomer, I thought. She'd entered the undergraduate art school at age twenty-seven.

In my room, I called and left a message for Lieutenant Felker, my room number and the name of the motel. I recorded a brief message on Ray's answering machine. I called Inside Moves and learned the owner wasn't in. I asked the woman who answered the phone whether the gallery represented the works of Kathleen Kelly. I was told it didn't, that her paintings were currently being sold at a working-artists gallery at Forty-fifth and State Line.

It seemed odd that Kathleen's work wasn't sold through Inside Moves, if Rosalinda and Warman had been "bringing her along."

A secretary answered Metro's work number. I filled him in on how I'd spent my first evening back in Kansas City. Metro confessed that he might have heard that Rosalinda had sold her house, but insisted he didn't know for certain.

"You knew she was married."

"I tell you, man, she left us all behind long ago."

"You could have said so."

"Yeah, I know, I know. But it was ticklish, Rooster. You got to admit that. Ray, too; he kind of had this thing for her right after you left town the last time."

"Ray?"

"Right. She, uh, well, you know, she kept coming around and drinking with us. You get the picture, Rooster? I mean, you weren't here."

I didn't have a thing to say.

"I think she missed you, Rooster. She really did."

"Did you know Kathleen Kelly?"

"Naw. Check with Beth. The name sounds familiar, but I can't place her."

I finally came around to the tough questions.

"You wouldn't have any cops placing bets with you?"

"That's touchy," Metro said quietly.

"It's important."

"Are you really a suspect?"

"So it appears."

"And you didn't kill her?"

Was I supposed to laugh? I didn't.

"Okay," Metro gave in. "What do you need?"

"Autopsy, forensics."

"You don't need a cop," he said. "But you may need an interpreter. Let me call you back."

"Fine," I said. "You wouldn't have a second number for Ray by any chance?"

"For you, Rooster, anything. But the only way to get hold of Ray is to find him. He won't answer the phone and he never plays back his messages. Look, if he's not at his house, make the rounds. Hold tight, though, for a couple minutes, okay?"

I watched a golden-bodied fly walk off the edge of the motel dresser. It looked like a miniature Mercedes SL going over a cliff. A man can dream, can't he?

I looked up Joseph Warman in the phone book. He wasn't listed. Neither was J. Warman. But Rosalinda Morelli was. The number didn't match the number Felker had given me. The phone book listed Rosalinda as living in a house on Ward Parkway. She'd either kept her name after getting married or she'd moved into the house ahead of the wedding. Ward Parkway didn't come cheap.

Taking a leak when waiting for the phone to ring is as certain to elicit a response as lighting a cigarette while waiting for your food to arrive in a restaurant. I zipped up and grabbed the thing on the fourth ring.

"Just as I thought," Metro sang, "they did it here. KU's one of the two best morgues in the city."

"The autopsy?"

"On the nose. I can have photocopies of all the paperwork by the end of the day. You want to meet?"

"Sure, but I've got a few things to do. I might not be able to nail down a time."

"No problem. I'll be at Jack's for supper. I've got my Tuesday collections. I'll be hanging around."

"That's fine. Say, you wouldn't be able to *walk* over, would you?"

"Oh, I get you. Yeah, sure. Look, it's in the lot behind the bank. I'll drop . . . no. Could you come up and get the keys? I'm in committees all afternoon. I'll leave them with Nancy."

"I appreciate it, Metro. By the way, what kind of car you got these days?"

He laughed. "You've been gone longer than I thought." I forgot to ask Metro if he knew anyone who drove a four-door green Ford before hanging up. I replaced the receiver and stared at it. Then I snapped it up and rapidly dialed the number Felker had given me.

No one answered after six rings. Feeling just like Moses this side of the Promised Land, I was relieved. I wasn't afraid to see her. I just didn't want to do it over the phone. Any charm I possessed involved seeing me in person. I'd rather watch someone walk away than have her hang up on me.

Dialing the number brought a knock on my door. I figured it was Felker or a couple of his subordinates. Others on the Metropolitan Squad would want to interview me themselves. I pulled back the edge of the motel drapery and caught my breath. I would have been less surprised to see Santa Claus.

Rosalinda wore a raspberry-colored halter-top sundress, and a tan shown off by the spaghetti straps over smooth, square shoulders. She looked purposeful and anxious, as the breeze swirled the full skirt behind her, emphasizing the length of her legs. She looked purposeful and anxious, like a hot wind come to blow your house down.

We said very little.

Our bodies surrendered inhibition the moment we embraced. I untied the straps of Rosalinda's dress, then lifted it over her almond-colored hair. She wore a pair of white cotton panties and no bra.

We pushed ourselves against each other. We pulled each other against ourselves. Rosalinda made love with one ankle-strap sandal on, but had at some point removed a large pendant-and-hoop earring, which had no mate, and placed it on the table between the beds.

As so many times before, I imagined her full lips swelling around the small, hard cries that lifted from the very back of her extended throat. My eyes were closed. There was no flirting in our lovemaking. We didn't even get her panties off, but wedged the cloth to one side. She opened like a sliding glass door and closed with me inside. There was a fireplace in the warm den and I meant to throw myself into it.

A rotten thief, I left something behind. Rosalinda said not a word while we were making love, though I repeatedly called out her name. It could have been any name to fit any woman. Because there was only one woman in my life and I was finally, fitfully, and most intimately with her. Her name was the way a tongue moved forward and back, the way a tongue moved touching another tongue, the way muscles press and slid and trap.

Her name was the sound your body makes trying to leave its bones behind by rushing from your locked-open mouth. And for a moment, she was near-sighted, almost cross-eyed, our eyes watching our eyes, inches apart. It was the face of lovers. I could see my face dancing there in the cornflower blue of Rosalinda's eyes.

If our lovemaking had been a song, it would have been a drum rolling without rhythm, a heart opening and closing around blood without beat. It was a song the lyric of which sounded like scream.

Rosalinda in the bathroom, I wished we'd taken more time. I wished I'd slapped our bodies together like multiplication tables. I wished I'd taken the occasion to rediscover the inches of her body, one by one, to have tasted the salt sea where a bead of moisture had surfaced upon her flesh. But there would be time for that, I believed, a lifetime perhaps. Her coming here had told me all I wanted to know.

I listened to a siren outside on the streets rise and fall and rise again. My body trembled at its memory of an individual moment shared between us, a moment remembered from a mere moment ago. An aftershock. I thought of the siren as someone rushing to someone else's emergency, while my emergency had just begun.

I wanted to keep her here. Forever. Shoot the clock. We could send out for a month's groceries. We could catch salmon if we ran the bathtub just right. We'd bring in birds for music and erect a treehouse in the corner. We'd cover ourselves with sunlight and night. We'd have a hundred babies to rule the jungle by.

Fatality is biology's way of saying all bets are off. But you couldn't die in a life like that. I wanted to tell her if she didn't leave we could live forever. I longed to tell her that.

Rosalinda walked in from the bathroom, her body in place. She'd rinsed her panties in the sink and left them folded over the shower rod. I swear to you, I could hear them drip. She picked up her dress, a puddle of raspberry on the carpeting, by bending at the waist, as a dancer might, and poured the pool of cloth like water over her blond, her translucent, her golden amber hair until it was a dress covering her once more.

Man, if you could see the future, you could see it in Rosalinda's hair.

Five

I'm not one to go talking about tits and ass. But, let me tell you, they were there. If you rubbed oil on your palm and pressed it upon Rosalinda's breast, you'd feel her heartbeat rise to the surface until it burned between your fingers. You couldn't get a hold of that. But you could touch it; and when you touched it, you never wanted to stop.

Juliet could have taken lessons from my true love locating her shoe. Rosalinda found it and sat down with her golden back to me and slipped the sandal on.

I relaced the bodice of her sundress because Rosalinda seemed intent on being dressed.

"You always were the expert, Rooster, but this was good-bye."

I said nothing in reply. I was expert only in knowing finally when the best had come along. I leaned up and kissed her shoulder, engulfed in scent. She could call it what she wanted. She didn't fool me with the good-bye crap. Rosalinda could say it with her mouth, with her back turned, but she couldn't say it with her eyes.

This was the homecoming I'd been waiting for. Call-me-

Joe Warman didn't have a chance in hell. Or in Missouri, for that matter.

"I'm serious, Alton," she said. "We had to do this. No sense putting it off. But you can't take one giant step backwards and have everything the same."

"Not the same," I admitted. "Better. I want everything we had to be better."

Rosalinda rose from the bed to sit on the other bed, facing me. She'd redone her makeup. Her eyes were clear and deep and she seemed like a woman now, seemed in control. There was a frightened little child inside of me, inside of all of us, sitting somewhere just inside our skin, inside our fears.

"Cover yourself, Rooster," she asked, glancing away. "You look, I don't know, vulnerable like that."

"It doesn't hurt," I said. I pulled the bedspread over my lap, my legs. A faded detail I noticed during our lovemaking was a horizontal bruise on the inside of each of Rosalinda's wrists, where the skin is tender, holding pulse.

They might be scars from an attempted suicide. I was saddened by the thought. The narrow, red bruises were cries for help. I was here, dammit. Didn't she see *that?*

"You were always very sweet to me," she said softly. "I appreciate that more than you know. All my memories of you are good ones even though you left."

"You're on your way up, Rosalinda. I'm here to see to that."

"You know, Alton, it was probably good for me. Your running off."

I closed my eyes and breathed in deeply. I didn't want to hear what was coming. Of course she felt this way now, unfaithful in her marriage. But tomorrow or the day after tomorrow, or someday next week, she'd realize. . . .

Rosalinda brushed back her hair, cut now six inches below her shoulders. Her gesture was casual. Her hand didn't shake.

"You're repeating words of a speech you memorized," I claimed. "That was what you planned to say, so you're saying it. I'm in love with you. And always have been."

I stared straight away from her. Just now the truth could not be trusted were I to watch her reaction. I felt her hand on my arm.

"Come on, Alton. Be honest. This is your midlife crisis. It's not love. You're just reliving the past."

"Bullshit."

Rosalinda picked up her purse from the dresser, watching me from the foot of the bed.

"I came to say good-bye," Rosalinda repeated. "You are very dear to me, Alton. You're a very dear friend."

"Friend?"

I held out my left hand, fingers together, thumb closed. I held out my left hand slightly cupped.

"When I put my hand between your legs," I said, "it fits." I held it toward her. "I can read your heart."

"It's your heart, Alton," she shot right back. "Not mine. I'm a picture in your high school yearbook. My life is mine now. Things have changed."

I thought about Beth's description. Rosalinda didn't have doll eyes. I did.

"You keep a babe flat on her back, she don't see nothing," I said from out of nowhere.

"I'm standing up, Franklin. I'm standing up and I'm walking out that door. And when it closes, it's over."

"What about the children?" I tried.

She stared at me, confused, her light blue eyes widening. "What children?" Rosalinda asked.

"The ones we were going to have," I said.

She stared hard at me, then laughed. "It almost worked, Alton. You do have a way, I'll give you that."

At least she wasn't reciting all that claptrap about there being a perfect woman for me and how she sincerely knew I would find her one day. Where do women get that speech? There was one thing Rosalinda could say to make me happy again. And it wasn't going to be today.

She was at the door. If I said anything, I might weep. I stared instead. I breathed through my mouth.

"Marc's out, you know," Rosalinda said. "He's looking for you."

I nodded melodramatically.

"He's been calling, Alton. I won't let him near the house."

"What's Joe think?" I managed to say.

"Good-bye, Alton." Rosalinda closed the door, leaving behind her panties, her scent, her me. I stood up. I cried. I broke the lamp.

Doll eyes, my ass. I wanted this woman every night. Of course she still loved me, I concluded, walking across Rainbow on my way to Metro's office at the medical center. Another five years she'd want those kids, all right. Nobody could look at Joseph Warman and seriously consider procreating the type.

My wardrobe was limited. I wore yesterday's blue jeans and a blue Chicago Cubs T-shirt. Metro was out. As he'd promised, he'd left the keys to his car with the secretary. Metro's personal transportation was a '58 two-tone Ford station wagon. How could I have forgotten?

The floorboards in the back were rusted out and you could hear bits of sticks and gravel kicking up inside the car from time to time over the laboring rear end of the classic automobile. They put big engines in vintage station wagons and this one would cruise at a hundred and twenty miles per hour. Of course, it would require several miles of straight road to get it going that fast. Just what Kansas was made for. As it was, I spent a half hour negotiating a right turn.

The radio worked. I wasn't sure about the brakes. Navigating Metro's yacht-size classic along Rainbow Boulevard, I heard a break-in newscast that KCMO firefighters were battling a blaze in the 4400 block of Fairmount.

"Firefighters successfully contained the blaze. Yet, they were unable to save the home at Forty-four-twenty-nine Fairmount from complete destruction."

That explained the sirens. In the city, you learn not to ask for whom the sirens roll, lest they roll for thee. The building referred to was Rosalinda's house. Our house. Kathleen Kelly's house.

It was the strangest feeling, a clear sense that Rosalinda's making love to me had burned down the house. I would have settled for a thunderstorm, a small earthquake in Istanbul. If we'd only slow-danced around the motel room in our underwear, perhaps the house would still be standing.

Caroline Rooney reported for WDAF Radio that the homes on either side of the razed structure suffered only minimal water damage. No one had been injured. No one had been at home. It was too soon, she added, for firefighters to determine whether arson had been involved. Hell, I knew right away. And, I guessed, so did they.

My mother would have told you that having sex with a woman married to someone else would end with this result. The firefighters should have turned their water hoses on me. I was walking around with a chest full of hot coals. If you'd looked closely when Rosalinda entered my motel room, you could have seen the embers in my eyes. Were my fingers to touch paper, they'd leave behind ashes.

I wondered how long it would take the media to realize the fire was at the same address as yesterday's dead body. Somebody had cooked those six-ninety-nine-a-pound steaks of mine on purpose. And I'd be the first one Lieutenant Felker asked about it. Truth was, I felt responsible.

And Rosalinda, I feared, was vulnerable. A person who'd go back and burn down a house would definitely not recoil from having to kill again. Even his wife.

Standing on the peeling paint of the porch floorboards, I knocked. Someone moved around inside the house, but no one was answering the door in any big rush. *Come on,* I wanted to say, *hurry it up, will you? I'm on fire.*

Things were happening too fast. Ray Sargent, Jr., wasn't one of them.

Ray's dining room served as his office and, in turn, his office served as his living room. He sat at the dining table, which was his desk. His typewriter, though loaded with a blank sheet of white paper, wasn't turned on. The table top supported a disarray of newspapers, books, empty beer cans, a coffee pot, two full ashtrays, and the butt of a deer rifle.

"You've heard about the murder—" I began, pacing, speaking quietly.

"That's not the worst of it, Rooster," Ray interrupted, speaking too loudly. "I've developed a fondness for natural settings, the more rural the better. Actually, it's more an absence of setting. It's very difficult to write about."

"Unless you go there," I commented, deciding to play along.

"Right," Ray jumped back in. "Right you are. I've been working on this article for two months now. I'm calling it 'The Middle of Fucking Nowhere.' But I don't know really where it is, you see?"

"Have you ever been to Wichita?"

"I was thinking maybe a little north."

"Nebraska then," I shrugged. "You've got the whole state to write about."

Ray rattled on about his proposed column and I let him. He was clearly hiding something and simultaneously keeping me from saying anything. Someone else was in the house.

Ray's connections in the city ran the gamut from freelance locksmiths to pay-by-the-piece art thieves. His father, a retired police officer, operated a very successful private security company. Sargent Security's headquarters occupied a multistory glass building in Corporate Woods. Clients were the rich and famous across the nation, including numerous politicians. Banks relied upon Ray's father for their security systems and analyses.

Ray had worked for his father's company briefly as an operative, serving subpoenas and providing routine domestic surveillance. But he rejected his father's enterprise as a career and finagled his syndicated travel column by writing articles and sending them to newspapers for free use until his reputation built.

The younger Sargent found himself occasionally sucked into private investigations in the city. Because of his father's reputation, people who could not afford the fancy corporation often sought out Ray Sargent, Jr. Perhaps he was a bit of a pushover. Or maybe it was in his blood.

Ray continued talking about no place in particular while he scribbled on a scrap of paper, finally handing it to me.

"Say, your dad quit the business yet?" I asked while he waited for me to read the note.

"He's waiting for me to come around," Ray said somberly. "I haven't quite managed to convince him that I'm a writer and not a junior private detective."

"Maybe he's read your stuff," I tried. Which is exactly what I was doing. His note said:

Beth's upstairs. She called in sick today. She's scared. The police talked to her about the Kelly murder. Don't say anything. Help me get out of here!

I did.

"You should learn to smoke, you going to get this nervous," I said through gritted teeth as I eased Metro's wagon into the traffic on Rainbow.

"Murder bothers the pee out of me," Ray confessed.

"How do you feel about arson?" I was waiting for the

rear end to respond to having been put in forward gear. It finally did, with a clang you could hear in Baltimore.

"Arson?"

"Rosalinda's house burned down."

"When?"

"About fifteen minutes ago. I need an alibi."

"On Fairmount?" Ray asked, reminding me Rosalinda now lived elsewhere.

"Yup."

"Where you found the body?"

"Yup."

"And you're the suspect, naturally. Idiot cops."

"Don't make fun of your family," I requested. Family's important where I come from. Besides, you can take it from me, Ray's dad isn't a cop anymore. He's an entrepreneur. In thief lingo, that's a person who makes money from thieves without risking the crime. Mostly, Ray's father made a good living thwarting thieves. But not always. He and I had done a little business in the past.

"No can do," Ray said. "The alibi, I mean. The catch is Beth. She might fess up the next time she talks to the Metro Squad and admit she was avoiding them by hiding at my place. Or, say she's afraid for her own safety to the point she asks *them* for help. Either way, it's a no win, Rooster."

"Maybe I won't need it. After all, I'm innocent."

It was Ray's turn to shrug. "That's worth something," he said. "But it won't buy you lunch."

Six

At Jack's, it was early enough to get a booth. We had a pitcher going.

"You want to start with the fire?" Ray asked.

"The murderer did it," I said, pronouncing fact.

"The whole thing smells organized, Rooster."

"I don't know about that. But I need some information about the fire."

"Okay. Forget the guy you see on TV. He's the information officer. A good guy, but he won't tell you anything that's not already in the paper or on TV."

"Next."

"Try Pat McElroy. He's in charge of arson investigation for the fire department, the Missouri side. Tell him I put you onto him. He'll confuse me with my dad and you'll get everything the police get."

"Know anyone with your father's company who might do a little free-lancing?"

"Such as?"

"Someone who might have a bit of listening technology

at his disposal, who might not worry too much about invasion of privacy."

"Everyone worries about invasion of privacy. But yeah, you better let me make a call on this one. Got a quarter?"

While Ray was using the pay phone at the back of the bar, I choked on a sip of beer. It was as if the muscles in my throat were fibrillating. My face tightened and turned red as I made my way through a fit of coughing. Aftershocks I decided. You never knew where love was going to hit next.

What I was choking back was what Metro had let slip about Rosalinda and Ray. I'd have to say something. I was old enough to wait.

"The guy's a little squirrely," Ray said when he came back, "so don't let him in on anything."

"Squirrely?"

"Thinks he's a spy. Anyway, he'll meet you tonight. You're not going to like this, Rooster." He paused to fill our glasses. "He wants to meet you at the Fairyland. Nine o'clock."

"On Prospect Avenue?"

"I told you the guy's a little weird. My guess is it'll cost you a grand."

When I didn't react negatively, Ray went on.

"His name's Steve Ruddick. Don't be put off by him, Rooster. He knows his stuff."

"Fine," I said. "Why don't you fill me in."

"Fill you in?" Ray asked. "On everything?"

"Start with Rosalinda."

"I think you're the one who could fill me in," Ray claimed.

I waited. Ray shifted in his seat, glanced up, then down. "Look, you got ten years on me, Rooster. You know what's what."

I stared hard at Ray. He had thin, dark eyebrows, a strong bridge to his nose. Doe eyes. There was a tiny white bump at the edge of his left eyelid, a separation in the lashes.

"Okay, okay," he protested. "So, Rooster, she got weird. Then she got snooty on the old crowd, you know. That's about it. She starts running in new circles, marries this dude who's got big bread and who's ready to back her plans. . . ."

I glowered. He wasn't going to say it.

Ray studied his beer, then spoke softly, apologizing.

"I just couldn't figure a way to bring it up yesterday, Rooster. You were so positive about getting back with her."

"You couldn't *mention* she was married?"

Ray shook his head. There was something else he couldn't mention. That he'd gone to bed with her after I'd left the last time. I'd decide later whether it needed mentioning at all.

"If it's any consolation, Rooster, we weren't invited to the wedding. It was back East somewhere. Virginia or Maryland. It's not anything anybody ever talked about. You've got to comprehend, Rooster, how thoroughly Rosalinda left us all behind."

He should have been around when the house was on fire, I thought.

"Tell me about Beth," I requested.

"What's there to tell?" Ray asked, relaxing, relieved to get off Rosalinda.

"What has she got to do with all this," I said. "The police questioned her?"

Ray took a breath. "She and Kathleen were friends. The cops gave her a good grilling. Seems there was a party at Kathleen's house Saturday night. The cops wanted everybody's name, what they said, how they acted, who left and who stayed—"

"Were you there?"

"No. Beth's about it as far as people we know. The rest were struggling artists, I think. Or dealers. You know, that crowd."

"Warman?"

"Yeah, and Rosalinda. Her gallery was sponsoring Kathleen or something like that. The house was part of the deal. Anyway, it makes sense that Warman would have been there. Kathleen had sold her first work for real money. Seven or eight grand, I heard. It was a celebration of her, uh, success."

"What's he do? I mean besides spend money."

"He's retired from back East. All I know for sure is he dabbles in objets d'art and antiques. And art galleries, of course. You aren't going to like this, Rooster, and try not to make too much of it . . ." Ray trailed off.

"Go ahead," I said.

"He's retired CIA. He was only a department manager or something, not an operative, and he retired young. His family has money since the Mayflower and they always collected art."

"What's their address?"

"I don't know the number offhand, but I can show it to you. Warman's Kansas City house is in the high fifties on Ward Parkway."

"He has another house?"

"I'm just supposing. Maybe he's got an apartment in Paris or a gentleman's farm in Pennsylvania. All I know is, we're talking real money here, the kind that never dries up."

We drove south on State Line in the Batmobile. I mentioned Kathleen's gallery at Forty-fifth Street as we rumbled by. Ray agreed it was worth checking out, agreed it was odd that Joe and Rosalinda weren't showing her at Rosalinda's gallery in Westport.

Before turning east on Fifty-fifth Street, we motored by the Carriage Club's pool and tennis courts on one side of State Line, the rolling fairways and greens of the Mission Hills Country Club's immaculate golf course on the other.

Mission Hills was a Kansas-side suburb and was once listed as the richest *per capita* income community of its size in America. This distinction was based mainly on the Halls, the family who continued to control private ownership of Hallmark Cards. The Halls had built and also owned Crown Center, a couple fancy high-rise hotels, as well as both Swanson's and Hall's Department Store on the Country Club Plaza.

I guess they have money. Recently the paper had run an article that mentioned the IRS was attempting to get a two-hundred-million-dollar tax payment from the estate of patriarch Joyce Hall. You figure it out.

The Missouri counterpart of Mission Hills was the neighborhood through which I piloted Metro's station-wagon-cum-tank.

The pedestrian islands diving the north- and southbound lanes of Ward Parkway were wide enough to double as municipal parks, complete with flowers and trees, fountains and statuary. The stately homes, as we approached Warman's humble abode, were half a football field back from the road and as large as their lawns.

One house at the corner of Fifty-Fifth and Ward Parkway contained thirty thousand square feet of living space. That's a lot of closets. Warman's house was as much as I'd expected: huge. The span of the lawn fronting the expansive two-story Spanish Colonial provided ample growing space for a variety of tall pines and old-world cedars. It was as if rich people owned more sky.

There was a brass sundial on a marble pedestal in the side yard, just outside the shaded jurisdiction of a columned portico. Side shubbery reminded me of hunkering animals with new haircuts. While the yard would have been a prime location for one or more of Rosalinda's sculptures, there were none.

Like so many large and expensive homes, Warman's house had everything but a front porch. The well-to-do did their loitering out back. In Warman's case, it was poolside, behind a tall privacy fence next to a tiled-roofed carriage house.

"Dobermans," Ray said. "You see them?"

There were two. I didn't give a damn. It would take more than a couple ear-clipped tail-bobbed dogs to thwart my plans. If Ruddick was a professional, he had a way to get around the dogs. My favorite was to open the gate, wait about a half hour, and come back after the dogs had gone. With some dogs, you had to go down the alley and whistle a few times before they would leave.

I turned the boat around and plowed north along Southwest Boulevard, between ironworks and body shops, liquor stores and salvage yards, heading under the overpass toward downtown. Ray had offered to drive Metro's motor home back to Jack's once he dropped me off to rent a car for the week.

"You wouldn't know anybody who could handle a theft?" I asked Ray point-blank.

"Besides you?"

"Not funny."

"Burglary?"

I nodded.

"Try a guy named Meza. Rick Meza, you know him?"

"Not yet."

"He's the king Wizard, the Harley gang on Thirty-ninth. Owns the block with the body shop and motorcycle repair. There's a new and used general merchandise shop on the other end. He's a KCK boy, but lives across the line as a ploy against potential prosecution. The guy fences a fair amount of stuff and could put you onto somebody.

"He owes me a favor, Rooster. You can call it in, I don't mind. But, listen, you've got to be careful. Meza's okay, but these other geeks will yank out your teeth with rusty pliers if you slip up."

"All right," I said, allowing Ray his moment of personal intensity. I didn't need a lecture on outlaws and the underground.

"Meza's okay," he repeated. "But those other clowns . . . just watch your ass, you know what I mean. And you may as well figure whoever pulls this thing for you will take whatever the hell he wants."

Yeah, I figured that. In my old line, we called it juice.

I parked along the curb outside the rental place, taking only two and a half parking spaces.

"There's one more thing," I said before climbing out. "Somebody called the cops."

"Is that why they picked you up?"

"While I was in the house, Ray. While I was in the house. I think someone followed me from Jack's. You know who might be parking a green four-door Ford with Wyandotte County plates in his parking lot?"

"I'll look into it," Ray promised. "Hope I'm not forgetting anything. You know I don't like doing this stuff."

"But you owe me one, Ray. For old time's sake, for me not saying a single damn word about you going to bed with Rosalinda. For me not asking how long you waited before getting her under the sheets."

"Metro," Ray muttered, shaking his head with his eyes tightly closed. "That son of a bitch!"

I rented a tan Camaro. It was an ugly color for a car, but would blend in with the normal traffic once it collected a little dust.

Now all I had to do was figure out the relationship between Ray and Beth. He'd let slip during our conversation that Beth considered Kathleen a best friend. I struggled to remember everything Beth had said to me yesterday. Best friends were confidantes. It was quite possible that Beth already knew the motive for Kathleen's murder. The question was whether Beth was aware she knew.

She had every right to be frightened. And my wager was she was frightened of more than the police. I wasn't particularly scared of anybody, but myself. I had things in mind you wouldn't want people you love to be thinking about.

Seven

The working-artists gallery was modest and small. The most remarkable thing about the place was how clean the windows were and that the awning out front had no rips or holes in it. No more than ten works were for sale. I couldn't read any of the signatures on the paintings. If the art on exhibit included a piece or two by Kathleen Kelly, her work was quiet, perhaps serene, and nothing at all to get excited about. The gladiolas, through the window, looked pretty much like gladiolas.

A sign on the door explained that the artists-in-residence were not to be disturbed without an appointment. "Sales hours" were from eleven A.M. to two P.M. on Monday, Wednesday, and Friday. Someone assumed, I reasoned, that art was something you bought for lunch. It was Tuesday and the tall reception counter up front was unoccupied.

I tried the door. It was unlocked. I stepped inside. From behind a barrier of Peg-Board wall, I could hear a radio playing.

Following the noise, I walked around the display of paintings I'd seen from the window and found four distinct work areas that made up the remainder of the gallery. The first two were standard painting setups, complete with easels and works in progress.

I'd taken a handbill from the counter. The gallery exhibited at an open house on Wednesday—tomorrow. Many of the galleries in Kansas City cooperated by holding show openings on the first Wednesday of the month, serving complimentary wine and cheese to a cadre of art students and young professionals who trooped from one gallery to the next, attempting to second-guess the local critics.

I'd need Meza sooner than I'd planned. I'd need Meza tonight.

Two large back areas were better lit. A young woman stood behind a long table, bending over her work, a brush in one hand. Across from her, on my left, was the fourth studio space. It was Kathleen's, I figured. It had been cleaned out. Damned quick, I thought.

"Excuse me," I said, using my friendliest voice. It comes out something like a drawl.

The girl looked up and smiled briefly. She was limitlessly attractive (women at work often are), though far too young for my romantic interest. Perhaps it was the lighting, but there was a brightness about her that reminded me of Rosalinda. Some carry around their own light. When they open their eyes, they'd wake you up in a dark room. This girl was one of them.

She had wide shale eyes, straight dark hair, broad shoulders, and incredibly smooth skin. Like paint, her skin was all one color.

"Hello," she said pleasantly but without looking up from her work again. "We're closed."

"I'm a friend of Kathleen's," I said.

"Oh, I'm sorry," she stammered. "People wander in and out. It's rather like being in a circus some days. We can't lock the door when we're working. Something to do with fire codes or insurance."

"Her work is sold here, isn't it? Someone told me . . ."

"Not anymore," she said, finally glancing back up. That southern drawl will get you cut off every time.

"They moved her stuff out," she added, with a sweeping gesture. She almost smiled at me, paused awkwardly, then looked back down at her work. Sometimes you get the most information by simply letting people talk. I didn't say a word.

"A Westport gallery is showing her tomorrow night. You can bet they're going to be asking quite a lot for her paintings. I was hoping to buy one, but now . . . well, the publicity and all."

"I'm Alton Franklin," I finally said. I approached her work table and offered my hand.

"Meg," she said. "Meg McNally. I'm always forgetting to tell people my name. Kathleen said I needed to work harder selling myself."

As if to demonstrate, she accepted my hand and shook it firmly. Her grip was strong. Meg was a ceramicist. There were flat square tiles on her table in makeshift frames of six and eight. She'd been glazing a picture on the tiles in one frame when I'd interrupted her.

"I'm nearly done," Meg told me, apologizing. "Let me finish up."

Meg took away her hand and only then did I realize I'd been holding on to it. She dipped a brush into a plastic jar of glaze. With deft control, she pushed the glaze across the surface of the tiles. The glaze, upon firing, would turn a color, a specific shade of life that only Meg knew at this point.

"This one's bold and abstract," she said. "I'm interested in the colors. Abstracts don't sell as well as pigs and cows do. That's what people want, pigs and cows, dogs and cats."

"And nudes," I said. Meg laughed.

"And nudes," she agreed. "I've never done a nude on tiles. Maybe I should give it a shot."

I was thinking about the bathroom floor. Blame it on the light.

"Mr., uh, Franklin?"

"Call me Alton," I said pleasantly. "Everyone I like calls me Alton."

Meg wiped her hands on a rag.

"I never heard Kathleen mention you," she said. "Were you at the party Saturday night?" Meg blushed upon asking the question. "Oh, I'm sorry, that was tactless, wasn't it?"

"Don't apologize," I insisted. "I got into town Monday morning. I'm the one who found Kathleen."

"That must have been horrible."

"You may as well know, Meg, that I'm one of the suspects in her murder. Even though I wasn't in town when she was killed, the police still believe I had something to do with it or that I know something they don't know because I was there first."

"The cops are paranoid," Meg claimed. "They probably think you threw out her diaries and washed all the dishes before calling them."

The idea of a diary was fascinating. Artists kept journals, I knew, wondering if Kathleen's had been burned in the fire. Probably.

I told Meg McNally that Kathleen's house had been razed earlier that day. Meg said she'd heard the sirens. "But I never really listen to the radio. It's just noise in the background while I'm working."

I asked if she knew Beth Rogers.

"She works at the bar on Forty-third," Meg said. "Jack's, I think. *That* Beth Rogers?"

"Short, blond hair, perky?" I asked, playing dumb.

"Yeah, that's her. She and Kathleen were, er . . ." Meg stumbled. "Close friends," she added hastily. Her eyes flashed to one side as she tripped over something she hadn't meant to say. Meg held back, assuming if I were a friend of Kathleen's I'd already know what she'd nearly said. If I didn't know, she wasn't going to be the one who told me.

Close friends. Best friends. Beth and Kathleen had been lovers.

"How come none of your work is in the window?" I asked to ease the tension.

"I'm new. My stuff opens tomorrow night. Why don't you drop by . . ." Meg paused, changed thoughts, and said, "I'm sorry. Everyone tells me I need to do that."

"I'd love to see your work, Meg. I've always liked porcelain. If it weren't so difficult, I might have tried it myself by now."

"Not that difficult. Just touchy. It's what I like to think of as the perfect cross between glass and ceramics. You can't treat it like either one or you come out with a gray lump of nothing." She smiled pensively at her own expression. "Will you really come by? It's my first show and it would be nice if there were a crowd."

"Wouldn't miss it. What's it go for?"

"Not a lot," Meg said. "I'm an unknown. If you want something, though, you can get it cheaper from me. I have some things at home I'm not showing that I'd sell really cheap to someone who likes them."

"Wouldn't it be better if I made a purchase through the gallery? That way you would demonstrate salability."

"I guess you're right, but most of the stuff in the show is pigs and cows. You like farm animals?"

I let a frown answer that one. "Did you stay after the party was over?" I asked.

"No," Meg said, giving the question very little thought. "Those parties give me the creeps. I always leave early. It can be a strange crowd and some of the people are, well, into things I don't care to watch, you know what I mean?"

"How long had Beth and Kathleen been lovers?"

"I'm not sure," Meg replied nervously. "I told you I'm new. I met Kathleen here and . . . I shouldn't be talking about this, but Beth and Kathleen were already friends when I met them."

. . .

"I'm sorry, sir, we close this evening at five and will remain closed for the hanging until seven tomorrow evening," the clerk in a black dress told me as I loitered among the current works on display at Inside Moves. *Closed for the hanging*, I pondered, picturing a cowboy dangling from the branch of a tree. She wore high heels. What the hell, a cowgirl would do.

While most of the Westport shops were open well into the evening hours on weekdays, the galleries all closed early in anticipation of First Wednesdays. They'd stay closed to hang their monthly shows through the day tomorrow. Paper covered the inside of the windows in an attempt to mount interest and to shut out the view of the mess until the show was up.

"I really must be closing now," the girl who worked the gallery floor insisted. "I can guarantee that the owners will not be dropping by soon."

"There's absolutely no way I can preview Kathleen Kelly's work?"

"I could be fired," she protested. "It was just delivered this afternoon. It's not even catalogued."

"We wouldn't want anyone to be fired," I said, stepping around her. Maybe it's the Chicago Cubs T-shirt that gets no respect. Maybe it's the Cubs.

"Of course, you're welcome to visit the shop tomorrow evening. Hey, where are you going?"

It was too late. I marched around the reception counter and into the back room of Inside Moves without so much as a glance over my shoulder.

The immense back room was stacked with various cartons, some laid flat on work tables. Kathleen Kelly's paintings were lined up along one wall. They obviously had not been crated for the trip from the gallery on Forty-fifth Street. Even in the dim light of the storage room, her work was striking. But paintings weren't what I'd come to see.

"Sir, sir!" the clerk called, her high heels clicking after me.

Two small, high windows in the back wall let in light from the alley. There was also a sliding metal door that I knew from my exterior survey of the building opened onto a concrete loading dock.

"You must leave at once," the young clerk bravely announced.

She was almost right. I ignored her and had a further look around. Sheetrock partitioning created an office in the back room. The door ajar, I caught a glimpse inside. Two chairs fronted a large desk. There was a round oak table and a filing cabinet.

If the desk had a locked drawer, then I wanted the contents. If the desk were unlocked, I wouldn't fool with it, and would satisfy myself with raiding the file cabinet. I may not know art, but I know what I like.

"I'm calling the police," the clerk sputtered, afraid to approach me. She spun in place and huffed into the outer room. I was outside in a minute.

I'd seen enough. Well, almost.

I keep my eyes closed when making love as a defense, I suppose, against sensory overload. I look into a woman's eyes while she's naked, pressed against me, and it's over. You may as well fold me up and put me in a paper sack you place on the curb for the trash collectors. Eye contact can be the most intimate contact of all.

Not that I haven't been known to peek.

What I'd seen when Rosalinda and I made love came back to me in flashes. The earring on the dresser, her splayed then fisted fingers, the pale and tender skin over the delicate inside of her wrists, which were marked with thin bruises or scars. Pinkish-red marks crossed her wrists. It seemed obvious to me that she'd tried to kill herself while I was away. I was saddened by that.

Driving along Westport Road, I saw Rosalinda's eyes and forced myself to picture other things. I'd seen Kathleen Kelly's work, had glanced at more than a dozen paintings in as many seconds in a darkened storeroom. Still, her art had left an impression on me.

It was bold stuff. There were female nudes, but not figure studies. Her paintings were a more direct display of female nudity. They were agressive nudes, if that were possible.

Brightly colored, Kathleen Kelly's women in oil exposed themselves in a direct manner you might associate with pornography. There was, however, a sense of purpose and power in their execution. The effect was of someone showing up at your door in a Halloween costume on Christmas Eve. A pirate stepping out of your shower, or a skeleton rising up from the backseat.

Eight

I flinched as I drove by the intersection of Fairmount Street on my way to Jack's. There was nothing for me there now but what was gone. I wondered if the Judas tree survived.

"I got a number for you," Metro said before I had a chance to sit down at the bookie's table. "Ray left it for you in my car." Metro handed me a slip of paper.

"That's not a car," I said. "Order me a glass," I added, feeling in my pocket for a quarter. "And a taco or three." It was going to be a long night.

Ray had written down the local phone number, the name Pat McElroy, and the words *After five*. A formal call, I thought.

McElroy was more than happy to talk. Ray, it turned out, had called ahead.

"No doubt about this one," he said.

"Arson?"

"More than that. Professional arson. Very professional. This baby didn't burn down. It was taken out."

"How's that?"

"Last year we had a house go just about like this one. Guy was operating a strip joint, you know the story. Just opened up and wasn't cooperating with the people who run that sort of business in town."

"Yeah." I encouraged him.

"So, one day they shoot out the windows. A week later somebody tapes a stick of dynamite to the guy's windshield. Car's parked right in front of the place. I don't know, maybe he was stupid or something; but in less than a month, everybody in town is waiting to see what happens. They take out his house."

"Fire?"

"Bomb," McElroy said. "It was a one-story job with no basement, a ranch. Not twenty feet to neighbors on both sides and the house is just missing like someone reached down and picked it up. There's a pile of smoking bricks no higher than your knee."

"Was he killed?"

"No. He was out of town by then. Must have been tipped. I guess he finally listened."

"You're telling me it was a bomb on Fairmount today?"

"Yes, sir, an incendiary. Blew out the entire basement. The rest of the house fell in on the fire, just sat there and burned."

"Same arsonist, you think?"

"Who knows? But they must have gone to the same bomb school and graduated at the top of their class. Both bombings were in the middle of the day and there's been a dozen or so just like them across the country. It's as professional and as expensive as arson gets. All our boys had to do was watch it burn and make sure the neighbors didn't go running at it with garden hoses. It's what we call a weenie roast, you just sit around in your gear and sing camp songs till the fire goes out."

"Was the house empty?"

"Yeah, of course. I thought Ray said it was your girlfriend, er, I mean, I thought you knew the house was vacant."

"Only making sure," I said.

"Don't get me wrong. People throw bodies into fires often enough. But there was no body in this one. It was just a piece of perfect work. Hell, the police were sitting across the street in an unmarked when the thing went off. Scared 'em shitless."

"I imagine so."

"Hey, don't tell anyone I said this, but the cops were there all along. Been there all night watching the house."

Somebody with connections and means beyond those of the average criminal had taken care of business. An arsonist that thorough and that unperturbed by the presence of the police not only didn't come cheap; he didn't come at all unless the right people asked. It had to be Joe Warman who apparently got whatever he wanted.

Danny Harrison was sitting at the booth with Metro when I returned.

"Rooster," Danny said as if he'd just lost a bet and was confused by the outcome. "Metro said you were here. I thought he was only trying to keep me out of his tacos."

"Help yourself," I offered. I slid in next to him. "You been elected to anything yet?"

Danny was a large man with curly blond hair and a boyish face that made him popular with women and with other men alike. He always wore dress shirts with the sleeves rolled up and a dark tie, topped off in the evening with a Royals baseball cap. The line on Danny was his shoes could be filling up with blood from a pair of busted balls and he'd hang around to shake hands with everybody before taking a ride to the nearest emergency room.

"Not till I'm married," he said cheerfully. Danny liked being around people and was totally and perpetually absorbed with a young and clever bombshell, Shelley Liptz.

Their on-again, off-again relationship left him plenty of opportunity to drink the evening away as a long-standing member of the After Hours Club.

"Lips still holding out?" I was being polite. To not ask about her would have meant I didn't care.

"Can you understand it?" Danny wanted to know, grinning.

"Blame it on youth," I said.

"Blame it on brains," Metro interjected.

Danny Harrison was the business manager of a Kansas public service workers union that included among its membership the KCK police department. He'd run for public office one day. For the time being, he stayed busy keeping people up and down the municipal ladder happy with their prospects. And he often had lunch at Jimmy's Jigger with men in expensive business suits, with men whose regular haunts were downtown on the Kansas side.

"Who's your cousin?" I asked when the waitress filling in for Beth brought another six tacos and a fresh pitcher of Boulevard to our booth. Danny knew *everybody* and the joke was that he claimed every woman in Kansas City was his cousin. When you called him on it, he'd walk over and introduce you.

"Wendy," Metro answered for him. "You know what's going on with Beth?"

I nodded. Nothing more was mentioned about it.

"Nothing like an entrance, Rooster," Danny said. "Being arrested for murder your first day back."

No one laughed.

"Metro mentioned it on the phone today," he went on. "I wouldn't have joked about it, but I called around. Our guy on the Metropolitan Squad said you weren't a viable suspect. They just think you know something. A guy blows into town and finds a fresh body, well, they know you didn't do it, *but.*"

"But I'm all they got."

"That's it, Rooster." Danny lowered his voice. "You may

as well know, too, that you're being watched from time to time. They're hoping to be there in case some heavy shit falls on you."

"Gee, I was just hoping to be breathing through my nose when it happens."

"They're not all bad guys," Danny insisted, the born politician surfacing. "You have to realize it's a big case in their books."

"Mine, too," I said humorlessly.

"Look, you need a place to stay?" Danny changed topics. "You have Shelley's house. She always liked you and since I'm staying there now, I wouldn't mind and I know she wouldn't."

"Give up your house yet?"

"Naw, my sister moved into it for a while with all three kids. I told her to make sure it stays in one piece and all she has to do is pay the utilities."

"I thought you got free utilities by now," Metro chimed in.

"It was too far to drive anyway," Danny rationalized, ignoring Metro's comment.

"You mean too far to drive in the morning to change clothes before driving back to work," I countered.

"I keep my clothes in the car when Shelley's in a bad mood. Otherwise, Rooster, I'm a piece of the furniture." He winked. "A piece of the furniture."

Danny was warning me in more ways than one not to try to move in on Lips.

"Congratulations, Danny," I said. "You look good as a couch."

"Save it for the wedding, bud." Danny smiled broadly under the brim of his blue ball cap.

We ate our tacos. Between bites, Metro advised betting against the Royals. I disagreed. I was home now and I would support the home team.

"I'll go for fifty," I said. "Straight up. No juice."

"No juice," Metro said. It was a side bet between friends. Danny didn't gamble. It was a lousy way to get elected. "Missouri's in charge of the murder." Danny told me what I'd already read in the papers. "I'd be careful, Rooster. Those KCMO cops aren't all on the side of the downtrodden, if you know what I mean."

"Yeah, right, and Kansas is as clean as bluebirds over the rainbow," Metro said.

"Sure," Danny responded. "Sure they are. They're union, bud."

When we finished eating, Metro and I excused ourselves. We ended up in the front seat of the rented Camaro with the dome light on.

"Tell me what's here," I requested.

"Okay," Metro said, taking a deep breath. He ruffled the papers from an opened folder on his lap. "The cause of death was pretty clear and they documented it. The bullet in the brain is plain enough, so they didn't go searching for strange poisons and the like."

"Caliber?" I wanted to know.

"Thirty-two. The rest is more like evidence. The condition of the body, let's see . . . Blood alcohol was point-two-three. That's very drunk. And there were traces of cocaine and barbiturates."

"She was knocked out," I argued.

"Maybe, but don't forget the coke."

"Time of death?"

Metro shuffled the sheets. "Uh, looks like . . . yeah, Sunday morning, something like that. Body was discovered Monday afternoon. She was dead at least twenty-four hours, maybe longer. And she was known to be alive Saturday night."

The night of the party, I thought. Eyewitnesses beat the crap out of medical evidence for determining time of death.

"You're off the hook on that one alone," Metro said, still thumbing through the photocopied paperwork. "Here it is, the weird stuff." Metro paused, reading to himself.

"What's that?"

"She had sex with somebody just before death. Two somebodies, it seems. For one, there was semen in the vagina. And it wasn't placed there after or during the murder."

"Okay, Metro. I got that."

"Rape's a possibility, but the evidence doesn't support a struggle. The rope stuff is here somewhere. . . . Yeah, here we go. She was tied to the bed, as you know, though not against her will. Slight bruising but nothing to suggest she fought against the ropes. And she was relaxed at the time of death."

"She didn't know it was coming," I said.

"Guess not."

"Could she have been unconscious?"

"I think so. It doesn't say here, but relaxed could mean passed out for all I know."

"So there's some sex after the party Saturday night, drugs, drinking, and she gets left tied up like that. Anyone else could come in later and blow a hole into her head. Or maybe she was drugged and tied in place."

We walked through Metro's marginal notes again.

"You said sex with more than one person, Metro?"

"I didn't write down the translation on that one. What it boils down to is there were vaginal secretions on the dead woman's face."

"I already heard that rumor," I assured him.

"Don't get me wrong, Rooster, you've been away for a while. But there's a similar rumor about Beth these days. I think Beth and the dead girl knew each other."

"I think you're right," I said.

"You want to keep this paperwork, Rooster, you didn't get it from me. Okay?"

"You can burn it. I got what I need." I flipped off the dome light. "You know this guy Rick Meza?"

"Yeah," Metro said. "I mean I know who he is. Some local dude who heads up a motorcycle gang. I think it's Hispanic, on the Kansas side."

"Think I can do business with him?"

"Yeah, sure. He's a better politician than Danny from what I hear. Make sure he's on your side first."

"Got you."

"And be careful. Meza's probably all right, but those biker guys live in a whole 'nother world."

I asked if Metro knew where I could get my hands on an unregistered item of protection.

"I can't mess with that stuff, Rooster. First bust, a bookie gets probation. Throw in a gun and who knows?"

"I understand." I did, too.

"You sure you want one? The cops are going to be all over you for a while."

"I'm sure."

"Try Meza then. That's the kind of thing he's supposed to be good at. He's probably got someone trying to sell him a gun for breakfast every day. Speaking of which, you got plans tomorrow morning? Ray and I are hitting the breakfast bar at Shoney's around seven if you're up."

Back inside Jack's, we watched the Royals on television. Danny sat with us at the bar, getting up from time to time to say something to anybody who came in the door. The game was tied in the third when my thoughts drifted to Rosalinda.

Joe Warman was obviously in charge. He'd backed her gallery. He'd backed her fancy new life in a fancy new house on Ward Parkway. It was his life. It was his gallery. And it was his murder. I could hear him telling me, "We're bringing her along," when he spoke of Kathleen Kelly last night.

He had her paintings. The paper would play up the murder tomorrow. It would be big news, lurid stuff. The first day a crime is reported in the press, it's the bare facts. The next day, the papers play up all the sensational elements to compete with the disco news on local TV channels.

Would her paintings sell for fantastic prices because of her grisly, sexy murder? Maybe. If there was money to be made from Kathleen Kelly's murder, Warman was in a position to make it. That thought left a sour taste in my mouth, a taste I couldn't spit out.

Before I left I remembered to ask Metro if he knew anyone who drove a green four-door Ford.

"You've seen one somewhere, Rooster?"

"Yesterday," I said. "The parking lot out back, I think."

"Could be anyone." Metro shrugged. "You catch a face?"

"No. I'm just trying to figure out who called the cops when I went into the house."

"Don't look at me," Metro said offhandedly. I hadn't previously thought of that.

Nine

Steve Ruddick was late.

An unmarked Dodge with blackwalls and no chrome fell in behind when I left Jack's. The Dodge lost interest as I drifted through eight different parking lots in Westport. Now I was waiting it out in the overgrown and bottle-littered parking lot of the defunct Fairyland Amusement Center wedged in among the other vacant lots, storefront churches, and pornography shops on south Prospect.

Closed now for several years, the Fairyland had once been Kansas City's largest amusement park. Weeds had taken command of the rutted gravel lots on either side of a fence that was itself in sore need of repair.

The night had cleared but the moon had yet to rise above the dinosaur skeleton of the dilapidated roller coaster track. Dilapidated and defunct, my dream of the future with Rosalinda was in about the same shape as the Fairyland. I wondered what I might rescue of the dream, if I could reach in and snatch her away intact from the middle of all this.

Were I able to do that, I'd bring her here on a warm September night. Only light bulbs would be strung from the carnival booths. Light bulbs would outline the Ferris wheel. There'd be meat on the dinosaur bones, noise on all the rides. And we'd dance under the stars to Jay McShann or Bennie Moten orchestras, who regularly played the Fairyland. Sway and tap our feet to the Kansas City Blue Devils.

Hell, I'd even wear spats.

Amusement in the heyday of the Fairyland was as simple as a place to take a stroll. Today, I was not amused by the way things were turning out. When I was a kid, you got twenty-five BB's to shoot the red heart out of a white piece of paper at the carnival gallery.

Whose heart was the target now, I wondered. Mine or Rosalinda's? I remembered the arcade machines. I'd put a nickel in one in 1962 and out came Annette Funicello on a three-by-five card autographed *Sincerely yours.* Tonight I felt sincerely lost, sincerely left out.

My future had been burned out from under me, had been married, had been murdered in cold blood. I'd be damned if I'd admit it was too late for the most important battle to be fought. I would resurrect the dead by lightly touching the skin on the back of her neck. I'd bring Rosalinda back.

I cared about Kathleen Kelly's death as much as I ached over the ruin of my own heart's intentions. There is a duty in seeing to it that someone who so badly needed it, the man who'd murdered her, was caught. I'd stumbled upon an obligation and I'd see it resolved. I'd shoot Joe Warman if I had to.

I hoped I had to.

Then I'd carry Rosalinda off on horseback to the music of a carousel. So much for the past, I decided. It's the future that has the power to last. The moon grows full, turns thin, goes out . . . and comes roaring back. Me, too. I'd get up the strength to do what had to be done. My immediate future pulled into view in a Chevy van under the shadows of the dead and dying Fairyland.

Ruddick was black, bald, and fat. He wore a three-piece suit. I climbed into the van and offered to shake hands. Ruddick instead touched a finger to his eyebrow and said, "Have we done business before?"

I certainly hoped not. The last time I was in town my business was stealing cars.

There was a way, he told me, that Warman's phone could be easily tapped. We decided on an external device that required no monitoring.

"It can go up tonight, if you want," Ruddick said. "The only risk is somebody will discover the box and walk off with it. That happens, I have to charge you cost."

"That's a deal," I said.

"Otherwise, we record a cassette of everything that goes over the phone. Nobody listens to it but you." Ruddick paused for emphasis. "Because you're the one who picks it up. Once she's in place, it's your operation."

I preferred it that way.

"Let's go look," Ruddick suggested and, without waiting for my reply, put the van into drive.

Lights burned in the windows of Warman's house on both the first and second floors. I liked to think of Warman and Rosalinda in separate rooms on separate floors. He was bent over a large desk, plotting murder. She was near an upstairs window, her hair ready to tumble toward me on the lawn. She was by herself in the castle, thinking of me, of our past together, and of our future once I rescued her from all this.

We selected a spot for the box on the backyard fence.

"We put it on the utility access side and that way you can't get busted for trespass," Ruddick said. "You get caught picking up the cassette and you say you just saw the thing and wondered what it was, all right?"

"Okay. You need me to watch?"

"Hell, no, Rooster. I'm not the one who hooks it up. There are dogs inside that fence. You come back in an hour and it'll be there is all I can tell you." Ruddick gave me a small handful of replacement cassettes.

"We're going to use the power from the line, so the thing will run forever. What were you thinking of, a week?"

"No more than a week," I said.

"You let Ray Junior know when you're done and we'll pick up the box."

On our way back to Prospect, I asked Ruddick how much to pay him.

"You don't," Ruddick said. "We end up in court, I didn't take a dime from you. You give it to Ray Junior and he'll see to it from there."

"That's fine, but how much?"

"Pay me what it's worth to you. Ray Junior can tell you the usual range."

Once Ruddick had maneuvered us into the Fairyland parking lot, I thanked him for his services.

"Forget that. But you should know, just in case you don't, that I'm clean on this. You're on your own and, well, it's serious if you get nailed tapping a phone. It's federal. I wouldn't leave any fingerprints on the box."

He let me think about it a moment, then added, "If this guy we're tapping hired that murderer, all I can tell you, Rooster, is good luck."

"I don't believe in it," I said. "But thanks for the sentiment."

I bought an eighty-nine-cent Butterfinger.

It was the sugar I was after. I carried the candy bar and an extra-large Styrofoam cup of coffee to the counter of the convenience store at Thirty-ninth and Main. Two girls in brightly colored tights and contrasting short-shorts held open the glass door for me as I left. I tried not to stare. One of the girls had orange-and-blue striped hair.

Approaching State Line on Thirty-ninth, I turned on the

radio to learn the Royals were going into the bottom of the eighth tied three all. I parked the Camaro on the side street where Meza's block began. A small bar on the north side of Thirty-ninth was known among locals as a blind pig, a place to buy drinks after legal closing time. It was here, according to Ray, that I could get in touch with Rick Meza.

The bar was long and dark and nearly empty. It smelled of old beer and bad deals.

At first I thought she was deaf when I asked the woman behind the serving bar whether she knew where I could locate Meza. After a thoughtful pause, the extraordinary length of which might have been determined by the number of times she'd abused recreational chemicals, she lazily pointed to a large man leaning against the jukebox, watching two other sharpies shoot a game of eight ball.

The man had thin, wispy hair and looked to be at least seven feet tall.

"I'm looking for Meza," I said, standing directly in front of Kansas City's first runner-up in the national Goliath lookalike contest. A gorilla at the zoo had taken first honors.

As with any dangerous animal, I tried to show no emotion. I held perfectly still. Most of the tall man's front teeth were missing. If they had room for one more on Mount Rushmore, this face wouldn't be it. The guy was so ugly he was his own mountain.

Like the woman behind the bar, the tall man was taking his time to respond. Either that or he was ignoring me altogether. This was the fellow the other natives stretched across the mouth of a gorge so they could each walk across. His open Levi shirt exposed a chest tattooed with a black star inside a red triangle. It was the mark of membership in the Wizards Motorcycle Club.

"Ray Sargent, Jr. sent me," I finally said. "Are you Bodyguard?" That was the name Ray had given me for Meza's right-hand man.

The monolith opened his mouth, but he might have only

been attempting to breathe. It made my teeth ache just to look at him. I remembered what Ray had told me about rusty pliers.

"Across the street," Bodyguard eventually replied, brushing past me and striding to the front door of the blind pig. I followed, but not too closely. Around the back of the Wizards Motorcycle Repair and Body Works, I was told to wait in the alley. I couldn't entirely convince myself I was not being set up for a mugging.

Meza was a short, handsome Hispanic with swept-back black hair and massive upper arms. His manner was that of a person with power at his immediate disposal, a man who was listened to and who therefore spoke softly. We didn't shake hands.

"You're Rooster," he said. "You know who I am."

Meza was expecting me. I explained exactly what I had in mind, that I needed someone who wasn't afraid of breaking and entering. I also told Meza the precise things I wanted taken and precisely when, which was now. Or soon after.

"This is that *murder thing?*" Meza wanted to know, before deciding that he was the man to do the job. I was invited to come along. I then asked Meza if he knew where I could buy a gun.

"You want to kill somebody or for protection?"

"Protection," I answered quickly, though I doubted my reply would make any difference.

"Two hundred dollars okay?"

It was.

Bodyguard stayed behind the steering wheel of the black '56 pickup truck, while Meza and I slipped out the back of the camper shell behind Inside Moves on Westport Road. We'd parked around the rear. Parking lots were full to the edges with cars that gleamed in the moonlight as if each had been polished and waxed for this very occasion.

Most of the people in Westport were on the streets, walking from nightclub to nightclub in couples and small groups, listening to the summer bands of Kansas City's most popular night district.

Shift change, I knew, was at midnight. With any luck, all but one of the assigned police officers were on their way to check in at the Linwood Station. The moon, high now in the southern sky, also lighted the steps to the loading dock. Meza carried a small crowbar and walked with a purposeful swagger up the concrete steps. The light glinted off the metal bar as he wedged its prying edge into the gap of the sliding door.

It was unlocked and gave without effort. Meza slipped quickly inside and I was right behind him.

It happens that doors are sometimes left unlocked. People get in a hurry. Adrenaline pumped through my system in big clots. My body wanted me to react with some sort of physical exertion, wanted me to jump up and down in place or to run around in circles.

I led Meza to the office door. It, too, was unlocked, but this didn't surprise me. It was like finding the bathroom door unlatched once you'd already broken into a house.

I hated burglary. It drove me nuts, gave me the sweats. I always saw people standing in dark corners. Stealing a car, you get in it and drive. The driving eases the tension. You can scream if you want to, play the radio loud, let your feet dance on the pedals. Breaking and entering, you walk around on tiptoes and practice not going bananas.

I turned on the flashlight and rifled the desk, stacking the drawers on top. None of the drawers was locked. This robbery was turning out to be as easy as raiding your own refrigerator, if ten times as scary.

Meza had it down pat. He used the crowbar to pop the locks on the two-drawer filing cabinet and I removed the metal drawers. They were heavier than I'd expected and I nearly dropped the first one. Meza helped me empty two cardboard cartons from the storage area.

"This shit worth taking?" he asked.

"To tell the truth, I don't know."

I wanted something on Warman. If it wasn't in his file cabinets, it wasn't. But I had to look. Meza and I loaded the two cartons with the contents of the filing drawers. I threw in a stack of loose papers from the desk. We each carried one box and set them down at the opening of the sliding door onto the loading dock. I'd left the flashlight sitting on the desk in the office.

"What's worth the bother?" Meza wanted to know, specifically. There was a tinge of excitement in the biker's voice that his soft, slow speech was unable to conceal. The jerk was enjoying this.

"Anything in the glass case up front," I said. "To the left. The back of the case is open. The smaller the better."

While Meza ambled through the darkness to the retail area of the gallery, I found my way to Kathleen Kelly's paintings lined along the wall of the large storage room. Blindly, I selected one, thinking of Meg McNally, and carried it back to our pile of booty.

My raging pulse refused to quiet as I waited for Meza to finish up. Eliot Ness, I was certain, was on the other side of the sliding door. Police cars had parked in a large semicircle around the loading dock, waiting to turn on their headlights. Bodyguard already swung from the gallows.

I studied the squares of light the rear wall windows cast upon the floor, watching for the shadow of a face to appear.

"The painting worth anything?" Meza asked, perhaps considering whether to take one or two for himself.

"Sentimental value," I said.

"Let's load it then and get the hell out of here."

I stood ground level in the alley and carried everything Meza handed to me back to the truck. A young man in a bright yellow sweater was throwing up, leaning an arm against the brick wall just beyond the pickup. He appeared to notice neither the truck nor me. Only the painting remained when I remembered the flashlight. Meza said he'd go back for it, still holding Kathleen Kelly's stretched canvas in one hand.

But it was only two seconds before Meza reappeared, obviously agitated, obviously on the run. He threw the painting toward me and in a single bound leapt from the doorway to the ground, a racehorse out of the starting gate. He slapped me on the back and yelled, "Go!"

I retrieved the painting and barely caught up with the truck that Bodyguard had already started and slammed into reverse. The pickup stopped abruptly and I ran around to climb into the back. I tossed in the painting. Before I could jump properly onto the rear bumper, we were off.

Pushing off one foot with as much strength as I could muster, I managed to bang my knee into the tailgate. A pain shot up my leg as I felt the full muscle of Meza's powerful arms, pulling me face first into the bed of the moving pickup.

"What the . . ." I muttered,

"Bomb," Meza said. "I don't know how we missed seeing it."

We tumbled clumsily, and for me painfully, over each other as Bodyguard spun the truck onto Pennsylvania, accelerating south. I cursed the stiffening pain in my knee.

"The office," Meza continued. "It was right there all the time. Whoever left that door unlocked was setting you up, my man."

No one knew about my plan to rob Warman's office.

"Are you certain it was a bomb?" I asked, still breathless, still rubbing my knee and trying not to fall over in the careening truck.

"A bomb," Meza repeated. "It was a steel toolbox with wires and a clock face on the outside. The whole thing was wrapped in silver duct tape. A bomb, Rooster, a bomb."

We heard the blast from four blocks away. I peeled off my latex gloves and tossed them with Meza's pair out the rear of the moving truck.

"At least we don't have to worry about the flashlight," I said. The bomb had taken care of that. I wondered what else it had taken care of. Obviously, someone hadn't minded destroying Kathleen Kelly's oils. Tomorrow was the exhibit opening and they hadn't been hung.

Ten

Bodyguard took another sharp corner and I tumbled into Meza once more, pounding my injured knee on the ridged bed of the pickup. I groaned.

"Hope all this paper is worth something to you," Meza said. "You just been pissed on by the big dogs."

"They were pissing on someone else," I countered. "I just happened to be there."

A man in my line has to fight against paranoia. No one knew I'd be visiting Inside Moves after hours. The place was bombed for reasons other than to catch me up.

The night filled with the sound of sirens as Bodyguard bounced us across State Line Road on a side street, heading in the general direction of the progress of the moon. Meza had a drop in Kansas, which turned out to be a house with the porch light on. The biker climbed outside, his pockets full, and told me I could ride up front now.

"Bodyguard'll take you back. But if I was you, Rooster, I'd find a place to unload that stuff."

It was professional advice. I attempted to express my appreciation for his assistance. I even considered apologizing for the bomb.

"Just tell Ray I don't like getting blown up," he said. Something in his voice or the sparkle of his dark eyes, though, told me the Wizard had enjoyed the close call. "You can tip the driver," Meza said, adding as an afterthought, "Don't let me be reading about you in the papers."

The tattooed behemoth said nothing as he drove me to Meza's block on Thirty-ninth Street. I left a C-note on the front seat and swear I saw the big man grin before he reached out and grabbed me roughly by the arm, keeping me from leaving the truck.

"The glove compartment," Bodyguard said plainly, releasing me. I opened the glove box and found a .38 nickel-plated revolver inside a cloth bag tied with a purple string. It was just like Christmas. Also inside the bag were what looked to be about twenty rounds.

It was only after I'd loaded the trunk of the Camaro and had slipped the unframed painting into the back seat that I realized I had no place to go. Too many people, including Lieutenant Felker, knew to look for me at the motel.

Perhaps one-thirty A.M. is the wrong time to come calling on a casual acquaintance you haven't seen in more than two years, even if Shelley Liptz and I had always seemed to like each other. I drove toward eastern Kansas City, Missouri, crossing streets the names of which are synonymous with muggings, stabbings, and rape. Urban homesteading, Lips had moved into a large Victorian home in desperate need of salvage. She'd always referred to her extensive remodeling efforts as "rescue" rather than repair.

Every woodworked corner of the old house had whispered, "Help me, help me," when she'd walked through with the realtor, Lips had said. Though she had planned to sell the house at a healthy profit, her efforts bolstered by municipal bond money, she ended up staying.

Lips was bright, young, and quite beautiful. At twenty-four, she worked as the director of computer information and training for a locally based freight company and earned well in excess of the average Kansas City salary. She deserved it. Whether or not she deserved me showing up on her front porch at this hour was another question.

I was relieved to see Danny Harrison's black Chevy Blazer parked in front of her house. The porch light was burning. I killed the headlights and pulled into the narrow driveway.

I unloaded the Camaro of its cargo, stacking the boxes and the painting at the rear bumper of Shelley's car. A personalized license plate I'd not seen before read *LIPS*.

A dog in the distance barked and refused to shut up as I climbed back into the car and parked it two blocks away on a one-way street. My left knee had stiffened. The walk might do it good. I stuck the bulky .38 revolver in my pants and hiked along the broken sidewalk back to Charlotte Street.

Lips wore a belted bathrobe, house slippers, and a broad smile.

"Rooster," she nearly crowed. "Danny said you were back."

Mumbled voices of a television program filled the background. I'd forgotten just how pretty she was. Her beauty was natural, without a hint of mystery to her features. Healthy and wholesome good looks, Lips reminded you of a lifeguard or a cover girl on skis. She reminded you of someone from Colorado.

We embraced and I was warmly reminded of her other assets. Bodies like hers accounted for the continuing popularity of dancing cheek to cheek.

Lips helped me carry in the boxes, telling me I should at least get a little red wagon if I wanted a mobile office.

Inside, I collapsed into a deep couch that must have been eight feet long, while Lips put on fresh coffee and opened a tray of ice. She'd made me remove my pants to assess the damage to my knee. I buried the revolver under one of the

couch cushions, then felt quite silly sitting there in my underwear.

She brought me the ice wrapped in a green towel, which
I in turn wrapped around my swollen left knee. Lips left the
television on but turned off the sound. She made herself comfortable in an easy chair facing the couch, her feet on an
upholstered ottoman. She said Danny was upstairs asleep.

"It looks great," I said, meaning the house.

"It should, Rooster. Everything's new. What you end up
doing with one of these places is building a new house inside
the shell of the old one." It sounded an awful lot like what
you did with yourself when the woman of your life married
another man.

Lips asked what it was like to discover a dead body.
Laughing, she asked if I'd touched it.

"The worst part," I said, "was that for a minute I thought
it was Rosalinda."

Lips studied my eyes as if she were looking for something
there.

"Aw, hell, Lips, it might as well have been Rosalinda," I
confessed, looking away. "Finding her married . . . I don't
know. It's wrong for her. I'm her real life and I'm the only
one who knows it."

"Sometimes you have to walk away, Rooster." She was
being sympathetic. I hate that.

"It isn't that way at all." I tried to explain. "Rosalinda's
in this world of shit. She stumbled into it. She's trapped and
doesn't know it. And it's like I'm the only man alive who can
rescue her. She'll die eating that upper-class shit if I don't do
something about it."

"You can't rescue someone who doesn't want to be rescued," Lips insisted.

"That's female crap! Independence, right? A woman
making up her own mind, not being controlled by a man.
Well, I'm all for it."

Lips looked skeptical.

"I'm not the man who's controlling her," I said.

"But you want to be."

"No, no, no. It's like she's been brainwashed, Shelley. They deprogram cult members all the time so they can return to their real life."

"You're her real life, Rooster?"

"Yes," I vowed. "Yes, I am."

Lips waited to make sure I was finished for a while, then said, "Coffee's done," and jumped up out of her chair.

"Shelley?"

She was halfway across the adjoining dining room. She turned and waited.

"I thought it was supposed to be easier to talk to women about this stuff."

"Easier, Rooster? Maybe it's just smarter." Lips stepped toward me, smiled slyly. "As long as a guy's getting his dick wet, he thinks everything's just fine. As soon as he isn't, it's the crisis of his life."

With that she was off to the kitchen. When God gave tits and brains to the same person, he created something dangerous for all men. Everything they write in *Playboy* is out of sync. Everything you learn in junior high locker rooms, in neighborhood bars around the pool table, in prison, is wholly worthless when it comes to women who are brave enough to think.

But that didn't mean she was right about this thing.

"It looks like Rosalinda," Lips said, staring at the painting. She handed me a cup of coffee and curled up with her own in the chair, her feet neatly tucked.

My knee was purple and lopsided and the ice didn't seem to help. I had yet to pay much attention to the painting. Now, I did.

"Who painted it?" Lips asked in a way that wasn't a compliment to the artist.

"The dead woman," I said. "There's a market for erotic art, I suppose."

The woman in the painting wore a chain of jewelry around her waist for a belt, an earring . . . and nothing else. Her mouth was slightly parted. She held open her exposed sex with the spread fingers of one hand.

It was a come-and-get-it pose, the kind of painting done solely for the prurient interest of a man. Rosalinda? The hair was a different color. I blamed it on poetic interpretation of the light by Kathleen Kelly. Otherwise, Lips was right, it was a rude portrait of Rosalinda. I'll be damned.

Rosalinda hadn't posed like this. It must have been Kathleen's lesbian fantasy. But Rosalinda had posed sometime. The presence of a pattern of three moles to the side of the nude's navel was as identifying for me as a matched fingerprint. And snug inside my jacket pocket was a loop-and-pendant earring that exactly matched the one in the painting.

Lips invited me to spend the night in the guest room. "It's a twin bed," she said, apologizing. "We did it up for Danny's daughter when she's here every other weekend or so."

She said good night and went upstairs.

I'd be staying up for the time being to rummage through the boxes on the floor. I turned on the lamp by the couch and found the telephone on an end table between the couch and wall. I dialed the number Lieutenant Felker had given me and checked my watch. When Joseph Warman, the flat end of Rosalinda's love triangle, answered the phone, I asked if he delivered and how much a large with extra cheese ran.

"Wrong number," he said and hung up. The call would serve as a general way to clock other calls coming in on the wiretap.

I was tired and my neck ached. My knee throbbed. I choked on the last sip of cold coffee and thought I'd never get my breath.

What I had ended up with was something short of the Brinks Robbery. Besides the disturbing portrait of Rosalinda,

there seemed to be little more than a desk full of bills, re-
ceipts, catalogues, letterhead, and embossed business cards
that showed Rosalinda and Warman as co-owners of Inside
Moves. One drawer of the filing cabinet had contained a mail-
ing list of customers. The items each had purchased or was
interested in were on a single sheet of paper in a correspond-
ing file.

You spend a few grand at Inside Moves, you get a Christmas card. I spent more time with these files than I should
have. There appeared to be nothing to help me pin anything
on Warman.

If he killed her to make a killing off her paintings, he
wouldn't have bombed the building they were stored in. Unless Warman was suddenly afraid of getting caught. Even rich
white people can go to jail for murder. Maybe my showing up
had thrown a scare into good ol' Call-me-Joe Warman.

Then I found a sealed manila envelope with the name
Kelly penciled on the outside. Inside were a large number of
Polaroids of Rosalinda posing nude. But none with her hand
holding open what it held in the painting. There were several
poses and numerous close-ups of her face, her fingers, her
most feminine body parts.

Despite everything, I found the photos sexually stimulat-
ing. I got up and put my pants back on, easing the left leg over
my bruised knee.

The Polaroids were an artist's study. They'd been taken
and used for Rosalinda's portrait, no doubt. And then returned to Warman upon completion of the painting. There
were too many photos of her hands for the photos to have
been taken for erotic pleasure alone.

I hadn't noticed the painting when I'd visited Inside
Moves earlier in the day. Yet, I'd only glanced at the works
lined along the wall. It made good sense, though, that the
painting hadn't been done for the gallery. It was likely a com-
missioned portrait and it was likely for the home. I considered

the possibility the canvas had been pried from its frame and stacked with the other unframed paintings for the purpose of being destroyed when the bomb went off.

I added to this the knowledge that I'd been told Inside Moves did not represent Kathleen Kelly's work. Warman had gone to some difficulty and probable expense for the right to exhibit her work in their monthly show. Or perhaps, I thought, to make certain her paintings were not exhibited elsewhere. Or, for that matter, exhibited at all.

Would Warman bomb his own business to destroy a painting? It was possible, I decided, especially if the painting directly linked him to the murder of the artist.

I plowed through the remainder of the paperwork from the files with the peculiar knowledge that every sheet of paper I touched was believed by Joseph Warman to have been destroyed. Ashes to ashes, I thought. I finally had an edge.

There were additional photos and slides, mostly of antiques, curiosa, and works of fine art. I was about to call it quits, my vision blurring, when I opened the last folder from the filing cabinet and stared blankly at three photocopies of a full sheet of U.S. postage stamps. I blinked repeatedly. The color photocopier had reduced the size of the original stamps so that the $8^1/2$ x 11 copies included all one hundred stamps. It was a photocopy of a full sheet of the one-dollar invert error.

I looked more closely. The margin plate numbers were in different positions on each photocopy of the sheet of stamps.

I chilled as I realized what I was looking at. These weren't three photocopies of the sheet of stamps. These were individual photocopies of three different sets of one hundred of the error stamp.

An invert error occurs when the paper is run through the presses upside down for one color of ink. A sheet of a hundred stamps is what collectors call a pane. The larger sheet is run through the printer and cut into panes. There would be four panes of any invert error, four hundred stamps.

I struggled to remember some of the details of the article I'd read in the paper concerning the one-dollar invert error. Only ninety-five of the stamps from the pane of a hundred the CIA employee had purchased from the post office were accounted for. The five, according to the AP, represented one each for the employees who grouped together to sell the bulk of the pane of one hundred.

If a single pane of one hundred stamps had reached public sale, it was likely the rest had slipped by the printer's eye as well. The article hadn't mentioned the discovery of the remaining panes of the error.

Warman's employment with the CIA had paid off. Someone was attempting to sell him the stamps. Warman may have been born rich, but if he pulled off a deal for the stamps, he'd be rich beyond the reach of the IRS. The profit for the middle man in this sort of deal figured easily in the millions.

I rechecked the annotated list of Inside Moves clients and customers and found no mention of a philatelist. I fell into a heavy sleep on the couch. When I woke, I'd blame my erotic dream of Rosalinda on the Polaroids or the painting. To tell the truth, I'd been having dreams of her for quite some time.

Eleven

The Royals lost again.

A young reliever brought up from Triple A to give the bull pen a September boost tossed four balls with the bases loaded in the tenth, pitching a walk that cost the Royals a game.

"What'd you do, piss off the Kennedys?" Metro asked. He pushed the *Star* across the table at Shoney's. The entire top half of the front page was a photo of the Westport bombing and the resulting fire. I read the lead. *"An explosion that shook midtown leveled one building and damaged two others at about midnight this morning."*

No one was inside the building at the time of the blast, according to the newspaper. I read on. Kansas City, Missouri, Chief of Police Robert Eulitt said the cause of the blast had not been determined.

"You're not mentioned," Metro said, watching me read. The waitress brought our coffees. She also dealt out two plates and a full complement of silverware.

I thumbed through the sections and scanned an item about a man who used an over-the-road tractor-trailer rig as a getaway vehicle after robbing an adult bookstore in east Kansas City. Then I found what I was looking for. An update of the invert error was a major portion of the *Star*'s weekly column on stamp collecting.

Existing examples of the misprinted one-dollar stamp had quickly increased in value once the story broke. John Reznikoff, of University Stamp Company in Stamford, Connecticut, acquired eighteen of the stamps for nearly one million dollars. "You have to understand the mentality of a stamp collector," he was reported to have said. "Since these stamps were filtered through the CIA, they're even more desirable. They have a history now."

It was the CIA angle that interested me. Warman had worked out of the Washington, D.C., area. A colleague, an active Company operative must have contacted Warman to sell the additional, unreported stamps. It could go both ways, I realized, official and unofficial. If it were unofficial, someone was getting wealthy; if official, though secret, the money would be used to finance your favorite CIA covert operation. Either way, Joseph Warman was the middle man.

The value of the error stamps was directly related to the number known to exist. Already, each of the known stamps from the sheet of one hundred was being traced. Nine of the stamps had apparently been used on outgoing mail before anyone realized the stamps were collector items. One stamp had been torn in half, destroying its value, when the CIA employees attempted to divide the stamps among themselves. That left ninety stamps in known circulation, most in the hands of dealers, including the eighteen errors Reznikoff had purchased.

The invert was being called a "profound discovery." I always thought a *profound* discovery was something more along the lines of a cure for cancer or the revealed existence of a tribe of subhumans living just beneath the earth's crust.

A philatelic investor was quoted in the article, saying there'd been only two legitimate inverts in the last seventy years. This was one of them. "The other," he said, "was the inverted Jenny, a 1918 twenty-four-cent U.S. airmail stamp with the picture of an inverted biplane. They currently sell for as much as $175,000 apiece."

The investor predicted the one-dollar candlestick invert to eventually bring as much.

Take that times three hundred, I thought.

Could the additional three hundred be slowly fed into the private marketplace in such a way no one realized the extra stamps were in circulation, right now they'd bring fifteen million dollars. The potential value was as much as fifty million. The information alone that three hundred more of the error stamps were in circulation would cause the price of the stamps, including the original ninety, to plummet. This was a secret I shared with Joseph Warman and whoever he was fronting for.

I couldn't tie it all together. The stamps had nothing to do with Kathleen Kelly's murder except that the stamps had something to do with Warman. And he had something to do with the girl's murder. I was sure of it.

"The police talked to me last night," Metro said.

I brought my thoughts back to the breakfast table. Metro had trekked to the bar and returned with a plate heaped with a variety of foods. He smeared jelly on a piece of toast.

"I didn't mean to cause you problems."

"I can handle the heat," the bookie said. "It's just that, well, you're getting on their bad side, Rooster. Danny can't help you out in Missouri."

I walked my stiffened knee to the breakfast bar. I'd had too little sleep to be hungry. I loaded my plate with fruit and melon slices.

"By the way, Rooster, why don't you let me know what you're up to today?"

"Why's that?" I asked, sitting down.

"I want to know which city blocks to avoid. I have what

psychiatrists call bomb-o-phobia." He grinned. "Dynamite-itis."

"Any luck with the green Ford?"

"Not really. You said it was a sedan?"

"An LTD. The big one. What do they call those now . . ." I fumbled.

"Crown Victorias," Metro said. "I'll dig a little further. Kansas plates, right?"

"Wyandotte County."

"Hell, Rooster, that should tell you something."

It did. Wyandotte was the county of KCK. "I was trying not to jump to conclusions."

"You might consider it's time to," Metro said, his dark eyes shifting away. "Before the conclusions jump on you."

"I don't have time for that rat-faced little prick," I said, meaning it.

"Maybe you'd better make time. Look here, if I know you're in town, if the cops know you're in town, if everybody in Jack's knows you're in town, then *he* knows you're in town. And in case you think otherwise," Metro said, lowering his voice, "Morelli's back in charge. Just like that." He snapped his fingers twice.

"I'll stay on the Missouri side." I shrugged.

"That's a fine idea, Rooster. But don't go thinking it's enough."

"Let me eat, will you," I mumbled.

"I don't know why Ray hasn't shown up," Metro said absently. "And Danny was coming by, too."

"Danny's sleeping in," I told him. "I spent the night at Lips's. Hey, I owe you fifty bucks."

"Or sixty-nine beers. It's up to you."

"What's the line on tonight's game?"

"You're a sucker, Rooster. The Royals are underdog, six and a half for seven."

"I'll take the Royals, a buck thirty."

"On the books this time," Metro said. "Juice is fourteen, all right? You're set to win a hundred forty."

We'd eaten and were on our fourth cups of coffee, about to give up on Ray, when Metro returned to the gallery bombing.

"So tell me, Rooster, you find anything last night before the place went up?"

"What do you guys do, call each other the minute I'm out of the room?"

"Something like that," Metro confessed. "I guess Ray called Meza to see what you were up to. Then I got a call from Ray. He keeps odd hours. He's doing a lot of work for you, Rooster, and I guess I'm feeling left out is all."

"You ever seen a murder?" I asked.

Metro shook his head. "Fatal car wrecks. Guys fighting, maybe one of them dies in the hospital later."

I couldn't describe the picture that flashed through my head of Kathleen Kelly's bound body.

"I laid down on the bed in my motel room yesterday, Metro, and it felt like I was her. It was the loneliest I ever felt. It's like when you're a kid and you're believing all this heaven crapola at Sunday school. Then you ask about your dog. Your dog, man, ain't going nowhere when it dies. They tell you that up front. Makes you want to kick the shit out of heaven."

"So what are you telling me?" Metro asked after a pause, trying to take the edge off.

"Don't go feeling left out. If I knew what to do next, I'd do it. If I needed your help, I'd ask you. But you don't want to get any closer to this than you already are, pal."

"Right," Metro muttered, not believing it.

"Unless you want to knock off Marc Morelli for me in your spare time."

"Not my line, Rooster," Metro said, chuckling. "But I'd chip in on it, you need another grand to get it done."

"Not my line either. I'd rather spend my time keeping

myself alive than getting someone else dead." Rosalinda, I thought, was the best being alive I'd ever been.

Metro straightened in his seat. "As I'm sure you understand, there is a great uncertainty in these matters," he said, using a formal tone. It was our code phrase that someone was listening. The sentence had come in handy over the years, used most often when somebody walked into Metro's office at the medical center while he was discussing point-spreads on the telephone.

Metro pointed with his eyes to a place somewhere over my shoulder. I adjusted the position of my swollen knee, then angled in my seat to see two uniformed police officers sitting at the counter, having coffee and pie.

"Don't get paranoid," I said. "Cops have coffee and pie all the time. It's part of their training."

"Not this time," he said. "Check out the lot." He nodded toward the plate glass windows overlooking the parking lot at Shoney's. It looked like a convention. There were two officers in a black-and-white parked directly behind my rented Camaro. Two other officers in plainclothes sat in an unmarked unit parked to the passenger side of my car.

I was two minutes from being arrested, I calculated, as the passenger door of the patrol car popped open.

My paper goods, including the Polaroids of Rosalinda and the photocopies of the inverted stamps, were in the trunk of the Camaro. I tugged my keys from my pocket and slid them across the table.

"Trade me," I said. "Once everyone is out of here, take the Camaro and vanish. There's some stuff in the trunk I need to have put someplace safe. *Real* safe."

Metro nodded, shoving the keys to his '58 Ford station wagon toward my plate.

If I didn't get up and going, the police would delay Metro, maybe take him in for questioning. Maybe take a peek in the trunk of his car. I couldn't let that happen.

"I'll let you pay," I said, climbing upright on my bad

knee. I worked the kinks out strolling by the officers eating pie. They waited till I was at the glass doors, then rose to follow me in tandem. Halfway to Metro's Ford, the two uniforms from the black-and-white caught up with me first.

"Are you Alton Benjamin Franklin?" one asked. It's such a nice name, I've never found a way to deny it.

The remainder of our conversation was brief.

"How 'bout those Royals?" I tried on the ride into downtown Kansas City, where Lieutenant Warren Felker was surely waiting to tell me one more time that I wasn't under arrest, but . . . Or, hell, maybe I was.

"Take off those handcuffs," Felker growled at the officer who ushered me into the interrogation room.

Felker watched as the cuffs were removed and my jacket was handed back to me. I was offered a seat at a long table with a tape recorder as its centerpiece. Six lovely aluminum ashtrays caught the glare from the overhead lights.

"Coffee?" Felker asked.

"I've had enough," I said, slipping on my jacket. I took the only chair at my end of the table, stretching out my knee as I sat. Three empty chairs stood guard against the far wall, behind Felker. Chairs had also been placed to either side of the conference table. It looked to be a tea party. Perhaps they'd have a cakewalk and I'd be asked to dance. Or one of those rented strippers you see advertised everywhere these days.

"I hope you don't mind the delay," the homicide detective said a moment later, excusing himself from the room. Alice and the Mad Hatter were a wee tardy.

There were no windows in the room, no windows, that is, that opened to the outdoors. Along the length of the table to my right was an observation window through which I could see only vague darkness. I thought I might be being secretly videotaped for inclusion in a high school crime prevention program.

Sometimes in life it's just you and your wits. Sometimes it's just you. Being in prison, you get good at eating clock. You get good at sitting in an empty room unable to leave. But you become frightened of it, too.

Pacing doesn't help. I invented a crossword puzzle in my mind. All the correct answers were *Rosalinda*. I came up with the questions I wanted to come up with. She was every woman I'd ever touched or been touched by. She was every woman of history when history was seen through my eyes.

Rosalinda had burned down Chicago. She'd built the Brooklyn Bridge, won World War II, and been elected president more than thirty-seven times. Rosalinda was every saint that ever lived, and the whore of every wandering eye. Rosalinda spoke soft words to Adam. And she never told a lie. Sometimes in life it's just you and your wits, which is always better than when it's just you.

Twelve

Eventually, I could perfectly describe the tint of blue of Rosalinda's eyes. Eventually, a small group of men filed into the interrogation room behind Lieutenant Felker.

They found seats at the table, except for Felker, who stood at the far end, facing me. The detective introduced a wide-faced man with freckles, who wore a trim summer suit, sitting to his near left.

"This is officer Pat McElroy," Felker said. "Arson investigator with the Fire Department."

McElroy allowed no trace of recognition to cross his features and neither did I.

I was then introduced to a squat man in an ill-fitting dark blue suit, sitting next to McElroy. James Muro, a KCK homicide detective, had been in the unmarked car at Shoney's. The dark eyes of the second-in-command of the Metropolitan Squad darted from me to a vacant space in a corner of the room.

To my immediate left sat an impeccably dressed man with a short silver mustache and a handsome tan. A very healthy-looking sixty with bright, clear eyes, Ray Sargent, Sr.,

wore his silver hair cut into short bangs. A gold Rolex decorated his left wrist and a silver pin in the shape of a pair of
handcuffs studded his lapel.

We'd met before. The ex-cop was the only one of the
group to lean forward and offer me his hand. I accepted and
returned the firm grip as a gesture of fair play before a fight
begins. Felker explained that the renowned private investigator had been retained by Mr. Joe Warman and was present to
share information with the police in their investigation of the
murder of Kathleen Kelly.

"I believe you already know Joseph Warman," the lieutenant said, introducing the man sitting next to Sargent, the
only other man at the table not wearing a tie. The Mad Hatter
had made it after all. My Chicago Cubs T-shirt paled in com-
parison to the pastel cashmere sweater covering Warman's
quiet chest. Rosalinda's cuckold had yet to look in my direction. It might spoil the pose.

"And this is Officer Morrison," the lieutenant added.
Felker's young assistant occupied a chair pulled away from
the table, behind and slightly to Felker's left, purposefully
siding with the officers at the table.

It was doubtful, I thought, that anyone at the table truly
cared about Kathleen Kelly in a humane sense, in a personal
way. Someone who'd known her, someone who had loved
her, Beth perhaps, should have been among the motley group
gathered in the windowless room. It looked to me instead like
people about to strike a business deal. Danny the politician
would have been right at home in one of the chairs at the
table.

Morrison turned on the tape recorder and returned to his
seat. Felker continued to stand.

"You are not under arrest at this time," he explained to
me for the record. "This is a, uh, fact-finding session. You
should know, Mr. Franklin, that what you say will, however,
be used against you if you have committed a crime."

"Thanks for the invite," I said, rubbing my right wrist

with my left hand to erase the flesh's memory of being hand-cuffed. "But somebody's missing."

I fumbled with my wallet, found a disintegrating business card, and flipped it onto the table. It landed against the ashtray being used by Ray Sargent. The private detective let it rest there until Muro finally reached across and picked it up. After a glance, he handed it to McElroy, who in turn passed the card to Felker.

"For the record," Felker said, "I will read at this time the card presented to me by Mr. Franklin." He recited the name, address and phone number of a Kansas City attorney who, for all I knew, might himself be in prison now. Or dead.

"As you may be aware, Mr. Franklin, you have the right to an attorney before you answer any questions involved in an investigation that might find you suspect of criminal actions. But you don't have to have an attorney for us to talk to you.

"You have given a statement to us previously without the presence of counsel and it was assumed you would continue to cooperate with the investigation."

I cleared my throat. He could assume whatever he wanted.

"We were hoping for your cooperation, Mr. Franklin. As we continue today, if you feel you cannot respond to something that might be said at this juncture, you are advised to discuss it with your attorney. Is that understood?"

Everyone seemed to be staring at their hands. Chairman was not a role that came naturally to Felker.

"For the record," I said, "Let it be known that I indicated I understood by nodding my head."

"Thank you," Felker said obliquely. "We're here, Mr. Franklin, to advise you. We have decided to proceed with issues today that do not at the present time involve the direct investigation of the murder for which you might be considered a suspect."

It was enough bullshit already.

"Shoot," I said.

"Do you understand our purpose?" Felker asked.

"As much as anybody," I said. "I also, for the record, understand that another suspect in the murder of Kathleen Kelly is seated at the table. Mr. Joseph Warman."

Warman shook his head slightly as if he were disappointed with, but not surprised by, my poor sense of honor and utter lack of diplomacy.

"Mr. Warman is not at this time considered a hostile participant," Felker said, speaking slowly. "Neither is he a prime suspect in our murder investigation."

"Who is then?" I wanted to know. "I sure as hell didn't do it."

Sargent chuckled under his breath. There was no prime suspect in this murder investigation as far as the police were concerned.

I was asked to repeat my version of the discovery of the body of Kathleen Kelly. No other version existed.

"And you entered the house at Forty-four twenty-nine Fairmount with no knowledge that a murder had taken place and without an invitation to enter from the owner of the home?"

"Yup."

Felker arched his eyebrows.

"I used to live in the house," I explained. "The spare key was where it always had been. The last time I was in Kansas City, I was not told that I would be unwelcome to return to the place I lived."

I watched Warman's reaction to my live-in relationship with Rosalinda. He seemed to redden slightly.

"I had not received word that my girlfriend had moved," I added, maintaining the stilted tone the tape recorder and the seriousness of the meeting seemed to require.

"You were gone two years and thought you could walk right back into your ex-lover's house?" Muro asked.

Yessirree Bob. "Believe it or not, gentlemen, I did."

We went through everything still again. All the while I wondered whether Ray Sargent was aware one of his operatives had bugged Warman's phone as a favor to his son.

McElroy discussed the bombings on Fairmount Street and on Westport Road when requested by Felker to do so. By now, everyone knew the second explosion was not the result of a leaky gas pipe. I had the fleeting desire to tell McElroy that he should be looking for the remnants of a toolbox. I remained confident that I was not a suspect in the bombings. I possessed neither the skill nor the means.

McElroy sat silently while possible motives for the bombings were bandied about.

"Isn't it clear that whoever murdered Kathleen Kelly had her house burned?" I finally asked.

"Not necessarily," Felker countered. That was all he said for the time being about motive. The bombings were, however, being taken quite seriously by the Metropolitan Squad. Warman, I learned, had requested police protection and it was being granted.

Then the time being was up and things got nasty.

"Let's suppose that just because a person is out of town that does not mean he isn't responsible for a certain crime that takes place in that town," Felker offered to the group, sitting down finally, facing me.

"Let's suppose a man in another city hears that his girlfriend has married someone else. Now, this man didn't really think an awful lot about this girlfriend . . . *until* she married someone else.

"He becomes obsessed then with getting even, of stealing her back. He suddenly leaves that other city without telling anyone where he's headed. And then, bang, he shows up just in time to call the police and say there's a body in his girlfriend's bed."

I stopped listening. Next, Felker was going to suggest the possibility that "this man" hired someone to bomb the house and the gallery to further threaten and harass the husband. Which is precisely what Felker did.

"Are you that man, Rooster?" he asked.

"I read in the paper about a guy who shot himself in the head because people were always asking him stupid questions," I said in response. "The reason he killed himself, or so his suicide note said, was because, while he was sick to death of being asked stupid questions, he couldn't keep from answering them. I can."

They waited for me to continue. I didn't.

"You didn't answer the question," Muro finally said, a bit angrily.

"You're absolutely correct, Officer. I did not answer the stupid question. If I did, I'd have to go home and shoot myself in the head when you're through here. I have other plans."

I felt like a cartoon character who'd just walked off the edge of a high cliff and was left to pedal empty sky with my crazy feet for far too many moments before the inevitable fall.

Felker changed the tape recorder. The meeting had been designed for the specific purpose of having me bleed all over the floor. Then things worsened. Joseph Warman decided to talk.

Trapped in a whirlwind of his own growing agitation, Warman reported finding an illegal wiretap on his telephone line earlier that morning. This was confirmed by police officers called to the scene. He was abruptly interrupted by Ray Sargent's jumping to his feet.

"I have to apologize for this misunderstanding," the silver-haired private detective announced, his hand on Warman's shoulder in an effort to both restrain and placate his client. "My company placed that tap to trace calls coming into the residence," he lied.

"Is that so, Mr. Warman?" Felker asked.

"Um, yes. I'm afraid I'm a bit edgy and I rushed to conclusions. Mr. Sargent and I haven't had the opportunity to communicate with each other prior to, uh, this meeting."

I wondered whether Steve Ruddick had betrayed me. But Ray Sargent would not have called the police to verify a telephone tap. Warman, I concluded, must have found it on his own. He'd likely only hired Sargent Security after finding the wiretap. Certainly he hadn't hired a detective of Sargent's ability to investigate a bombing which Warman himself had orchestrated.

Finding the bug had frightened Warman. That much was evident.

"Why would a man just up and abandon a situation, catch a flight without telling anyone, leaving his clothes and his car behind, whether or not he ended up at a murder scene?" Muro asked, ready to present a new theory and, no doubt, another round of stupid questions.

I could have told him it had something to do with love, a man's heart responding to a particular phase of the moon, the whim of a heart too long lonely; but, I decided, the cops prefer to come up with their own answers.

"A man who is being chased, Mr. Franklin?" Muro asked.

"Nope," I said.

"Haven't you made powerful enemies while conducting the affairs of your previous and current career?"

"I doubt it." None living. None living in Seattle anyway.

"I knew it," Warman spat, standing once more, surprising everyone by the fervor of his outburst. "This guy," he sputtered, pointing a trembling finger at me, "has recklessly brought all this grief upon my wife and me."

Such a quantity of blood had rushed to Warman's usually controlled face that I feared a projectile nosebleed at any moment. He was one hell of an actor.

Ray Sargent stood this time with his client, both hands on the taller man's cashmere shoulders. Together, they sat down again.

"Perhaps you can shed some light on this subject, Mr. Franklin," Felker suggested, ignoring Warman's accusatory outburst.

"No comment," I said. Then added in spite of myself, "It's a long shot and it doesn't follow."

"What doesn't follow?" Warman demanded to know, threatening to leap to his feet once more. "Someone wants you dead, mister. And they're destroying my life to get to you, they're destroying me because you show up out of the blue to look up an old girlfriend who wants nothing to do with you!"

"Why would my enemies attack you?" I asked.

Warman stood again. Both hands on the table, he leaned forward on straining arms. "They're using me to hurt Rosalinda. They're teaching you a lesson, asshole, by tormenting the woman they think you love. Dammit, Franklin, she's going to end up dead if you don't tell the truth before it's too late."

Warman was very convincing as a proponent of the theory that the best defense is a good offense. Or, as Bo Jackson once said when discussing his style as a running back, "It's better to give a lick than to take a lick."

I was on slow boil. I didn't mind being called names. The suggestion that I was the one putting Rosalinda in danger was, however, the limit. Warman was a worm, a murdering worm, and I silently dedicated my existence to stepping on this particular worm with the full weight of my boot heel.

"I'm through," I said softly. I stood up. "Someone around here should start telling the truth before it's too late. And it ain't me."

As I turned from the table, I couldn't resist the urge to speak. When your anger's on simmer it keeps you talking. It was my weakness. I turned on my bad knee to look back at the group of men.

"If you want my help, you've got it," I said. "I'll work with the police and that's for the record. But I'll be damned to pole-vault volcanoes in hell before I'll sit here and be cross-examined by a private citizen who has more reason to be a suspect than I do. And that's for the record."

I couldn't stop.

"Ask McElroy here how often an arson fire is purchased by the owner of the building. . . . I will not sit here and suck my teeth while this very man directs the blame toward me when he is ten times more likely to be your murderer than I am! For the record, Officer Morrison, please note that I am indicating Joseph Warman.

"And for the record, please remember to make a copy of the transcript for my attorney."

I wished I had one.

I held two fingers to my head and triggered my thumb. "Gentlemen," I said. "No more questions."

Outside, the sunlight was the color of weak tea. I limped slightly, still fuming, down the concrete steps of the municipal building, making my way to the taxi stand on the corner. A streak of contrail looked orange in the lousy sky.

"Challenges," my mother said, "make the man." She usually said this when I wanted something, say, a new pair of used shoes to skip school in that day. Maybe she was right. I was going to get that worm. And nothing could stop me now.

Thirteen

Ray answered the phone.

Then hung up immediately upon hearing my voice. When I redialed, Ray's answering machine had been turned back on. It may have been the first time he had answered his phone since installing the machine. He'd obviously been waiting for the call.

I found a clean but wrinkled button-down plaid shirt I'd crammed into my duffel bag for the flight out. You never know when a woman will want to eat out fancy. I put it on over the Cubs T-shirt. I didn't feel any safer, any less exposed.

The lamp shade on the dresser of my motel room had been removed from the plastic lamp standing nearby. Oops. My room had been searched. There were so few of my belongings in residence that only the lamp shade bore evidence of having been disturbed. The maid, no doubt, had been called into service once the beds had been tossed.

They couldn't have found anything that mattered. I'd left the gun buried in the couch at Lips's place. Metro was taking care of the stolen goodies from Warman's office. Rosalinda's loop-and-pendant earring was in my pocket. They could have taken a scalpel and cut me open from sternum to balls and not have found what they were looking for. Evidence did not exist that I had murdered Kathleen Kelly, because I hadn't.

Yet, it was the theory that the police seemed to be clinging to. Not a single person on the planet had known in advance I was coming to Kansas City. Whoever murdered Kathleen Kelly had done it without concern for me. The reason she was murdered had nothing to do with my being in Kansas City.

I was moving out of the room anyway. Once I'd used the facilities. Once I'd stretched out on the bed a while to relax and waited for answers to come to me. It was like waiting for the meaning of life to appear in your mailbox. Still, it was good to rest my knee.

I couldn't sleep and was undressed, readying for a shower, when the phone rang.

"Sorry about that, but I imagine you're tapped. I'm at a pay phone," Ray said.

"Enough said."

"About this morning," Ray continued. "I tried to get hold of you in time. When I drove down, I saw the cars outside."

"No big deal."

"If you still need a dentist, mine's out of town," Ray added before I could say anything else.

"What?"

"I'd suggest using the yellow pages. If you still need a dentist."

I listened to the line go dead. The reason Ray had called from a pay phone was the number I'd dialed could easily be deciphered by the dialing tones recorded on a tap. Should any number of things go wrong, that could be evidence held against him in court.

I retrieved the Greater Kansas City yellow pages from inside the top drawer of the motel dresser. I thumbed through the listings of dental surgeons, noting a handful of subspecialties. A second time through I found what I was looking for. On the inside margin on the second page of dentists, Ray had penciled a brief message. It didn't surprise me that Ray had found a way into the room. What are friends for if they aren't good at something?

The note was an invitation. It read:

Crown Center. Rm 626. 3 p.m. Discreet. Ruddick nearly caught! P.S. JW-CIA. Hugs & Kisses, R.S.

I pondered the significance of *JW-CIA* as I climbed into the tiled shower stall. Perhaps Warman was still an operative. Or perhaps he was being protected by the CIA. Ray could have meant to emphasize the connection between the man and the Company to guarantee that I remained alert. You put all these maybes on a plate and you still wouldn't have anything to eat for supper.

The hot shower would relax me enough to sleep, I hoped. I had a few hours to rest and no car parked outside to drive me away. I was out of the shower and leisurely shaving when someone knocked on the door. I wrapped a motel towel around my waist and, with a disposable orange-and-white razor in one hand, held back the drapes to see if my visitor by chance was Rosalinda.

No such luck.

"Make yourself at home, Lieutenant," I said, letting him into the room. "Assuming you're alone."

I returned to the recessed corner of the room to finish my shave. The shaving cream had run and spotted. It looked as if my face were clothed in spider webbing. I didn't care for the effect.

In the mirror, I watched Felker massage his untrimmed mustache at the edge of the far bed. He did not peer in the direction of the vanity alcove, but stared at something unseen on the blank wall above the bed.

"Lose your wheels?" Felker asked. Metro had the Camaro and I'd left the '58 Ford station wagon parked outside the restaurant. I rinsed the razor before answering.

"Took a cab," I said. I finished by shaving my chin. "You guys keep dragging me downtown for a tour, then you kick me out on the street."

I flipped the plastic razor into the wastebasket and rinsed my face. Taking the towel from around my waist, I wiped the remaining dried shaving cream from my neck. The air felt cool and clean on my jaw as I stepped back into the room and pulled on a fresh pair of wrinkled jeans.

"You see a doctor about that knee?" Felker asked.

"Inadequate health coverage is a hazard of my profession, Lieutenant." I was content to believe the knee would feel better if I could stretch it out for a few hours, although the bruise had darkened and actually looked quite frightening. It's the healing process that is always uglier than the injury itself.

"Things were overly dramatic this morning." Felker mumbled his version of an apology.

I slipped on the button-down shirt. Felker was staring. I gave him a look in return.

"I hadn't seen the tattoo," he said. "Take long to do?"

"About what you'd get on a second conviction for grand theft in Oklahoma," I told him, which was true. The jailbird artist who'd done the work had painstakingly colored each tail feather of the fighting cock tattooed on my chest.

"It wasn't my idea, Rooster." Felker continued blathering about the dog-and-pony show in the interrogation room. "We're under an unnatural amount of pressure on this one, the bombings and all."

"Ditto," I said. He should have seen Meza's face as the biker came flying from the dock door of Inside Moves last night.

"Warman," Felker said as if that explained everything. And it nearly did.

I transferred my wallet, comb, and pocket change from my other jeans.

"He knows how to work the system better than you, Rooster. Or myself, for that matter."

"From top to bottom, I take it."

"I'm somewhere in the middle, trying to do my job."

"You come by to cry on my shoulder?"

Felker rubbed his mustache. "Actually I came by to shit on your parade. But I'm determined to remain diplomatic."

I put on my shoes, bending my left knee as little as possible. I didn't know whether I was getting dressed to give Felker the impression I was preparing to leave or whether I had somewhere to go.

"You tap my phone?" I sat down on the edge of the other bed.

"That's for federal offenses," Felker claimed. "We're homicide. I did walk through this morning when you didn't come home. That's all."

"I thought this was a federal case, Lieutenant. What with Warman involved." I was fishing for information about Warman's link to the CIA.

"I thought about that," Felker admitted, apparently accepting the agency connection as shared information. "But the Kelly girl, she has nothing in her background to suggest their involvement. They don't even have a file on her."

"An innocent bystander," I mused. "You file Freedom of Information requests or are you taking somebody's word for it?"

"You may find this difficult to accept, Rooster, but we have our ways of gathering information, too. They're reliable."

Reliable perhaps, but not as satisfying as a routine B&E. I smothered an urge to tell Felker about the stamps. It was too good a hand to play it this soon and, besides, the cards were still being dealt.

"Look, we know you're up to something," Felker said. "Maybe it's time to tell us what you know."

"Sure. I know that Joseph Warman is up to his nuts in this mess. You want information, talk to his wife. She can tell you an enlightening thing or two about his activities is my guess."

"Out of town. She flew out yesterday on a buying trip. We'll talk to her when she gets back."

"South America? Cayman Islands?"

"Omaha, Rooster. And Des Moines. Warman provided us with her itinerary. They're cooperating with us fully."

"Cooperating? Is that what you call it, Lieutenant? I'd say he's leading you around by your foreskin."

"And just what is it you're doing to help out?" Felker was close to losing his temper. May as well join the club.

"For starters, I'm not hiring a fancy-pants private detective to second-guess you."

The lieutenant sighed heavily. "So Warman killed her, as far as you're concerned, and that's that? He bombed the house and he bombed his business and next he's going to cut off his friggin' arm and say somebody else did it. I don't know, maybe he'll set his nose on fire so he can blame you."

"I wouldn't put it past him."

"How long you been staking out my room?"

"When was this, Rooster?"

"Yesterday, I called in like a good boy, remember?"

"So what do you want to know?"

"Forget it," I muttered. I'd assume they'd been there all along. I'd assume the homicide detective knew of Rosalinda's visit to my cozy little nest with a number on the door. While it might help to account for Felker's insistence that I was the button to be pushed in solving this case, it wasn't damaging information. A tryst with Rosalinda might be evidence for my murdering Warman, but not Kathleen Kelly.

The problem, as I saw it, wasn't so much that I was a suspect in all this, but that Warman was being perceived as the victim.

"Warman's your man, Lieutenant. You should know that by now."

"I wish it was that easy, Rooster. I really do. I wish it was as easy as going after the guy who stole your girlfriend. I don't know, I have this fantasy of pinning some nasty crime on my high school principal, you know what I mean?"

I knew.

"There is something new," Felker said. He turned to look at me, his brow furrowed. He would study my reaction to what he said next. "The papers haven't got hold of it yet. We only found out today when the desk clerk called."

Aw, shit, he was talking about a body. Rosalinda? That crap about her itinerary was a setup. She was dead in the Omaha Holiday Inn Central? *What?*

"Guy named Ryan," Felker finally said. "Marty Ryan. Looked like an execution. Two shots to the head."

"Where? Kansas City?"

"Airport hotel."

"And Marty Ryan is someone I know, Lieutenant?"

"It appears he's our specialist, Rooster. His code name's Bloody Mary. An FBI check showed this guy is a known for-hire. One of the best. He's expensive, too. Works for the best and our fires match his established methods."

"So somebody with money is covering his tracks. Let's see, who could that be? You can't possibly think it's me?"

"Of course not," Felker said, letting my thoughts drift to the obvious.

"But . . ." I said for him.

"But, it could be the people who are after you, right?"

"Those people are figments of Warman's imagination, Felker. He blew that smoke up your ass to throw you off his. Wise up."

"No!" Felker shouted. "You wise up, Rooster."

He struggled momentarily with his seething temper, his fists clenching and unclenching, his knuckles going from white to red and back again. More sedately, Felker's emotions under the surface of his voice, the lieutenant continued.

"There's more to Ryan," he said evenly.

"Murder suspect on top of the bombings?"

"No, Rooster. That's just it. He has the same alibi you do. The two of you flew into town on the same damn airplane."

"Seattle?"

"Seattle," Felker confirmed.

"You don't think I'm part of his team, do you?"

"It's not clear yet. There's one thing in your favor right now, Rooster, but it's pretty slim. Ryan *lived* in Seattle. So it's possible he wasn't following you. It's also possible, though, that he was put on your scent in the Emerald City. You ever meet him?"

"Never. It's a coincidence, that's all," I said, thinking. "Okay then, forget Warman. Say some other guy with shitloads of money and/or connections has a good reason we don't know to kill Kathleen Kelly. He sets up the X-rated sex scene, or it was set up for him, and he pops her in the head.

"He goes home and gets scared. He flubbed something. Or he missed something. He makes a phone call. This guy Ryan grabs the first plane to Kansas City and does the job. Waits around another day for a repeat performance and . . ."

"And whoever hired him takes him out," Felker finished for me. "It's that simple, is it? You happen to be right in the middle of all this and have absolutely nothing to do with it. That's what you're asking me to accept, Rooster. Think about it."

"It's true." It was also true that it had to be Warman.

"Who called us then?"

"Anybody watching the place could have seen me go in. Ryan. Warman. Whoever was waiting to do the damn house, Felker. If I got pinned with the murder, good enough. When you let me go, they went ahead and blew it out."

"Who?"

"Specifically?" I asked. "Warman?"

"I stopped by, Rooster, to see if you had forgotten anything. Maybe you didn't want to talk in front of the others."

"Forgotten something?"

"We know you were in the gallery before it closed for the night. And it was blown up, burned. Ashes! You were in the house and then it was burned. More ashes! You get it, Rooster? You and this murder, it's one ball of wax."

"Nobody's blown up my motel room," I argued lamely.

Felker was about finished. I was finished before he'd arrived.

"Don't let me keep you," I finally said to break the silence. I lay back on the bed and wondered exactly why I'd quit smoking cigarettes. They were invented for moments like these. Beers were, too. Today was kind of special. The moment could use a few bad habits.

"I talked to Muro at length, Rooster." He was walking toward the door. "You haven't seen a big green Ford four-door traipsing around since you've gotten into town, have you?"

I didn't react outwardly, but any number of internal tissue masses tightened in unison.

"An LTD. Crown Victoria," Felker went on. "You want the license number, Rooster?"

I shrugged. At least I meant to shrug. I may not have moved at all.

"Well, you see that car again, Rooster, I'd dig a real quick hole and get inside it in a hurry. Make it a deep hole, while you're at it."

Muro was the Kansas-side member of the Metropolitan Squad. The car had worn Wyandotte County plates. I knew exactly what Lieutenant Felker was getting at. The pompous detective knew that I knew. Without another word, he was out of my room. Cops sometimes let things take their course.

Convicted felons killing convicted felons, cops could live with that. They'd arrest whoever was left standing, if they arrested anyone at all. My being dead wouldn't solve his murder, though. I had that on the high and mighty Lieutenant Warren Felker, KCMO PD. The green Ford sedan belonged to somebody in Marc Morelli's Kansas-side organization. I couldn't blame his sister, Rosalinda, for leaving town for a few days. I sure wish now she'd taken me with her. I wished it then, too.

I got up and closed the door.

Fourteen

A bit of sleep helped.

I had to wrestle myself awake. The cracks in the ceiling looked like a road map of bad choices. Choices I'd made all along. The cracks led to nowhere and indicated no way of coming back.

Rosalinda had been unable to undress in front of me with the lights on when we'd first met. I remembered what I'd been told about doll eyes and cautioned myself against creating a myth. I remembered the bruises, the thin pink scars on her wrists. Rosalinda and I were real, as real as the skin of her wrists.

This time the choice was easy to make. I could have blown town. Felker might have preferred it. But I couldn't do that. You stick around when you find what's real. I wouldn't leave Kansas City until Joseph Warman was either caught or dead. I wasn't going to let him get away with Rosalinda. I sure as hell wasn't going to let him get away with murder.

Good choices? Bad choices? Actually, all those choices are about the same. The thing is you've got to remind yourself once in a while that you're making one. A conscious effort, a schoolteacher once called it. Listen, I never stole a car I didn't mean to take.

I didn't come to Kansas City by accident and I certainly wasn't hanging around by chance. Maybe in a hundred years I could tell you whether it was a mistake.

Metro wasn't in when I stopped by to pick up the keys to the Camaro. I left the keys to his .58 Ford banana boat on the desk and used his phone to call a cab.

The department secretary crossed the hall and asked if I were Mr. Franklin. She had an envelope for me. Inside was a padlock key in a folded sheet of typing paper on which Metro had written two words, *Liptz's Shed.* It must have been where he'd stored the cartons of stolen paperwork from Warman's gallery.

Nancy, the secretary, invited me to wait. There was coffee if I wanted it.

"It's Wednesday," Nancy explained. "He'll be back to cover the phone." She winked. So much for Metro's secret occupation around this place.

On Rainbow Boulevard I stood at the curb in front of the steps to the medical center administration building. Watching two girls glide by in an MGB, I thought of driving off across the Kansas wheat fields in a red convertible with Rosalinda, her hair blowing in the breeze, her laughter carried on the wind. I shifted my weight onto my good leg.

Pershing Road was the southern limit of downtown Kansas City. I rode in the cab by the site of the Kansas City massacre. There'd been a civic endeavor when I'd left town to convert the monolithic Union Station into an aquarium. I pictured bug-eyed fish swimming by the third-story windows, a killer whale in the basement. Across the intersection was the Crown Center complex, the northern edge of midtown. It was easier to erect new buildings than to refurbish old ones.

I rode under the shadow of the Hyatt Regency Hotel,

where the skywalks had caved in, crushing a number of couples competing in a dance contest one Friday evening a few years ago. Crown Center rose above all this, high above its three-story waterfall in the lobby. Watching no one take advantage of a rooftop tennis court, I was hauled to the top of the Crown in a glass-walled elevator.

Alone on my way back down, I pushed buttons for the eighth, seventh, sixth and fifth floors. When no one was at the eighth or seventh floors, I stepped out on the sixth, but only after pushing the remaining buttons for the lobby and everything in between. Ray's note had said something about being discreet.

Prowling the hexagonal halls, I found Room 626, which, besides being a Mazda that lists for $15,699 without options, turned out to be a suite. Ray motioned me in soon after I knocked. The outer room was fitted with a table and four chairs, two easy chairs, a television set on a cart, a kitchenette, and a couch with a large, ugly head looming above the back cushions.

"You know Bodyguard?" Ray asked.

Bodyguard stood from the couch, awkward in his frayed denim jacket with the sleeves torn out. Ray suggested that Bodyguard wait downstairs in the bar.

"Rooster will come down when we're through here." Bodyguard stepped around me without quite acknowledging my presence and let himself out.

"Meza let me borrow him," Ray explained. "You want a beer?"

Ray opened two bottles of Boulevard Pale Ale from the minifridge in the kitchenette. I accepted mine and sat on the couch while Ray filled me in on what had happened so far.

"I know about Warman hiring Dad. We'll get to that. For now, you need to know that Meza has a message for you, for us."

"I know, Ray. He doesn't like being blown up."

Ray didn't grin. "The word's out on Metro and Shelley."

"What's that?"

"Somebody wants what they're holding for you. Word is to shake down Metro and hit Shelley's house. Somebody's willing to pay a bonus."

"Who could know about that?"

"Meza turned down the job, Rooster. So it's going to somebody else. I got in touch with both of them. Shelley's at work. Metro's waiting for you to pick him up at the med center. He wants you to go up to his office. Your stuff is in Shelley's toolshed. Bodyguard'll go with you to pick it up when you're through here."

"Who?"

"Forget that."

"Dammit, Ray, Meza can tell us. If Warman was having me tailed, he might know. But somebody had to follow Metro this morning."

"Maybe Meza can tell us. Maybe he can't. Either way, he won't. It's his livelihood over there. Those are vital connections as far as he's concerned. We're damned lucky he told me anything. He must have liked you."

"Charmed, I'm sure," I said. The wheels in my mind came to a screeching halt. "The cops, Ray. It's the KCK cops. They were there this morning. Off duty but in uniform, eating pie. They followed me out when I was picked up, got into some kind of four-wheel-drive truck. Instead of falling in line, they followed Metro to Shelley's house."

"Figures," Ray admitted. "Some of those guys will work for next to nothing. But they were just acting as eyes, Rooster. Someone else is running the show."

"What about Warman? Didn't you say CIA? He's still active, right?"

"First things first. I have a phone number for Shelley. She's staying at a friend's place tonight. You get in touch with her this evening and take care of her needs, okay? You might have to take her some clothes or something from her house."

"Sure," I said. I was old enough now to be patient. I

sucked back half the Boulevard. "You know what, Ray? You're good. You ought to do this full-time."

"I may," he said with a deadpan roll of his eyes. "Tomorrow, I'm over deadline for about the sixth week in a row."

"Warman killed the girl," I said. "I'm sure of it."

"Why?"

"I don't know."

"Okay, Warman. I called a guy at the paper, Rooster, and he pulled his morgue file. Like I told you, Warman's retired CIA, but nothing colorful. A pen-pusher, office management. He was a district supervisor, but mostly recruitment, materials, personnel. Nothing covert."

"That's what they all say."

"All I know is that was his job. He's covered in money that dates back to the Mayflower. Probably wanted to be a spy for the sport of it. He got in on his education and landed a management job. A few years go by and the fun wears off."

"Nothing covert," I reiterated.

"Nothing on record. He was in the wrong places. The paper did a spread on him when he came to KC to open the gallery with Rosalinda. His family always had an interest in antiques and fine art, that kind of junk. He's following a lifelong dream and something about the friendly people of the Midwest and how he hopes to bring in works as good as those you can buy anywhere in the world."

"Yeah, right, Ray. Retirement in the boonies. Big fish in a small pond. How long till that wears thin?"

"Money talks. Warman has clout in these parts, Rooster. Maybe he likes it."

"He also has your father on his side."

"Tell me about it. You should have heard Ruddick cuss. It was close. Warman found the tap himself, called the cops, then called Dad. Cops come out and stare at the box. Dad sends Ruddick out, right? He's the expert."

"So Ruddick covers his rear," I said.

"Exactly. Ruddick says to Warman that's sure enough a

tap, all right. And Warman wants to know if they can trace it backwards. No way, Ruddick tells him. And, Rooster, you want to know if Warman's a spy? Listen, he didn't even know the wiretap was self-contained. He thought it was broadcasting to a pair of headphones in a bread truck or something parked on a nearby side street."

"I didn't say he was smart, Ray."

"Ruddick takes the thing down, sweeps the house for bugs, and he's off. He told Dad it was somebody else's setup."

"Your dad believe him?"

"My dad hires the best, Rooster. He wouldn't second-guess one of his own experts. Not unless things double back."

"They won't," I promised.

"But you still owe Ruddick a fee," Ray said, reaching into his back pocket. He tossed something toward me. "You can play this at Metro's office."

I caught the baby audiocassette with my left hand. Ruddick had earned his fee.

Ray combed his hair with his fingers while I worked on straightening out my left knee.

"Listen, about my dad, Rooster. He'll fry your ass. Unless he decides Warman is jerking him around, you're going to feel the heat."

"So now I've got good and bad guys following me. Hell, Ray, I love a parade. With all those eyes watching nobody can do shit to me."

"Just don't count on my dad being one of the good guys. He doesn't go around breaking people's legs, but don't count on him being on your side."

"What can I count on, Ray?"

"Well, we've got one thing up on Dad. Ruddick's first job after pulling the Warman tap was to hook up your phone."

"He tapped the motel room? Hey, Ray, we've got us a direct line to the other side."

"Exactly. Anything you say on that phone will eventually be heard by Warman. Might come in handy. Trouble is . . .''

"Trouble is I have to keep the room," I finished for him.

"Or at least make it appear as if you're staying there."

"I'll unpack my bag," I offered. "The police are already watching it. They may as well have a party in the parking lot with the free-lancers."

"The other thing is I have to stay in the background. Deep in the background. My dad has our number. Your close associates are pretty well known and I'm definitely one of them."

"He'll leave you alone, Ray."

"I can't bank on that, Rooster. For all I know, Dad might enjoy seeing me in jail for a few months. Probably thinks it will help me see the light."

"Maybe he anticipates a plea bargain to move you into the family business." I finished the beer.

"Meza said you've got a gun."

"There's one nearby," I said.

"Better keep a string on it. When Meza turns down work it's likely to go to somebody mean."

"And I thought professional crime was only for nice guys, Ray." I filled him in on the Marty Ryan story.

"Bloody Mary," Ray mused. "I never heard of him."

"Funny thing is he's out of Seattle. Flew into town on the same plane I did."

Ray Sargent, Jr., arched his eyebrows.

"One-hundred-percent coincidence, Ray. I swear."

"Still, it's bad news. It means the more you find out, the more reasons there are for someone to shut you up. If they'll off him, they'll off anybody."

I believed I already held the information that was worth my life.

"What do you know about Marc Morelli?" Ray asked.

"He's out of jail and he doesn't like me."

"He's out of jail, that's for sure. Things have been shaking in KCK. You think he's involved in any of this?"

"Slim chance," I said. "I haven't had time to fart since finding Kathleen Kelly's body. He hasn't had time to set up anything. Nobody knew I was coming to town, Ray."

"You didn't send her a note? Call first?"

"Nothing. It was supposed to be a surprise."

"Well, he knows you're in town now. Probably found out a minute after you stepped into Jack's. Keep your ears trimmed, all right?"

I handed Ray my empty as he paced by. He strode into the kitchenette and came back with new ones for both of us. Then he turned his back to me and stared at the carpet.

"You sure you want to see this through?" he muttered. "Maybe you're trying to save a ghost, Rooster."

When he looked at me he had both hands on his bottle of Boulevard, squeezing it. He caught my stare. Just because Rosalinda went to bed with Ray after I left didn't make her a ghost. Just because she married some prick from back East didn't make her unreal or nonexistent.

"I'm not after memories," I finally told him.

Ray began to pace again. "There's someone here you need to talk to you." He paused. "Oh God, pal," Ray said quietly. "I hope you're ready for this."

Fifteen

Beth looked more tired than distraught.

She wore a cotton twill summer dress of bleached blue that seemed to swallow her. Her usually vivid facial features, including animated eyes, appeared washed and pale. It was clear she dreaded this.

Coming out of the adjoining bedroom when Ray opened the door and said something, Beth put on a courageous smile for my benefit. It soon faded. Her bottom lip trembled as she sat in one of the chairs across from the couch.

This had something to do with Kathleen Kelly. Beth looked to be mourning the death of a loved one.

"I'm afraid to talk to the police," she said.

"It may be necessary," I answered.

Ray slipped into the bedroom, leaving the two of us. She watched him leave with visible and increasing anxiety.

"They'll kill me, Rooster," she protested.

"Who *are* they, Beth? They're going to kill me, too."

"I know, I know," she said, nearly blubbering. "It's all my fault. I could have told you. I could have told you to leave them alone."

"Joseph Warman?"

She nodded.

"Who else?"

"Both of them."

"Warman and Rosalinda?"

She didn't reply.

"Look at me, Beth," I snapped. "Warman *and* Rosalinda?"

"Yes," she said softly. Her eyes wouldn't hold mine. "But there's more to the story. There's Rosalinda and Kathleen."

"Were you in love with Kathleen?" I asked, catching on. Was it possible Warman had killed Kathleen Kelly out of a fit of jealousy?

"Oh no," she said in the small voice of a young child telling the truth. "She was in love with me."

"And Rosalinda?"

Beth shook her head. "Warman had the money."

"I don't understand."

"Kathleen wanted something from Warman."

As we talked, Beth reminded me of the deeper feelings inside myself that showed so readily on her face, in the cast of her shaken gaze. I felt as if Beth were a part of me. The part of me that was frightened by the evil I'd seen in the world, in and out of prison, an evil I could neither properly understand nor predict.

"Kathleen wanted Warman to make her famous," Beth continued, "and sell her paintings for thousands of dollars. Well, eventually Warman did sell one of her paintings to a family friend on the East Coast. But it was an *influenced* sale, much the same as if Warman had put up the money himself. He was just leading her on."

Ray came back into the room. He walked to the fridge and plucked out another Boulevard.

"Have you told him about the party?" Ray asked Beth, approaching us.

Beth shook her head. She'd been working up to it.

"Kathleen knew something was going to happen," Beth insisted. "Something bad."

I waited for clarification.

"Saturday was this big party to celebrate Kathleen's sale. Everyone was at her house."

"The night she was killed?"

"Yes. Anyway, Kathleen had gone upstairs with Warman. She was high. I didn't think she knew what she was doing. But maybe she did. He kind of led her up there.

"Rosalinda stayed downstairs, like she was guarding the stairs. She stood right at the bottom. So, I figured they were snorting a little in the bedroom or something. I didn't like him, Rooster, but it was a relief. See, I wasn't in love with Kathleen and I think she'd been counting on me to stay over. It was her big night. It was her party."

He tied Kathleen to the bed, had sex with her, and killed her, I thought. Wouldn't someone downstairs have heard the gun? Maybe the gun came in later.

"Did you have sex with her?" I asked, recalling a detail of Metro's autopsy run-through.

Beth looked away. "No," she flatly stated. "I just couldn't, you know? I couldn't do it with her anymore."

Ray put his hand on Beth's shoulder. She looked up at him, gaining strength. I waited. I'd begun to guess wrong. It was best to let her tell the story.

"It was getting late," Beth persevered. "A lot of people had left. And those who stayed were pretty messed up. They were rolling on the floor, you know. Two guys squeezing up the same girl, taking her clothes off. People were really out of it by then."

"And you?"

"I was drunk but I was okay. I was kind of listening to music, wondering if I should spend the night or leave without letting Kathleen know. I didn't want to do anything wrong.

"Then Kathleen came downstairs and talked to me in the kitchen. She didn't say much, but she was frightened. I mean, she was real messed up, but frightened. She smelled like she'd just had sex."

Beth paused. I had no questions to ask.

"And then she kind of went ape shit. She pulled out a grocery sack and started filling it with boxes from the shelves. It was crazy. Macaroni and cheese, tea bags, stuff like that. She filled it to the top and gave it to me and told me I had to leave.

"We went in the dining room and then the front room and she started shouting that everyone had to leave right that minute."

"Did Rosalinda leave without Warman?"

"She might have," Beth said, and I hoped. "I didn't see her go, but she could have. Everyone was gone just like that. They were real pissed off at Kathleen and everybody left. Kathleen walked me out to the porch. I remember because she stumbled outside the door and almost knocked Rosalinda's sculpture over. And she told me to take care of the sack of groceries, said they were especially for me."

Kathleen Kelly hadn't been killed over a sack of groceries from the cupboard, I thought. But I must have been thinking too much. Beth read it on my face and turned pensive. Her voice was distant and dull, as if she spoke from a state of hypnotic trance.

"We stood outside for a long time. The air was cool. It was the first cool night and Kathleen was drunk. She rambled on about things. She looked right at the mailbox and laughed like she was crazy, then said it was going to make her rich. Then she told me not to let anyone have the groceries. That they were just for me. She kept saying that."

"The mailbox was going to make her rich?" I asked.

"I thought it was strange at the time, too. Maybe she was expecting a check in the mail."

"There was something else in the sack, Beth. What was it?"

"A videotape," she answered blankly, relieved that I'd

asked. "I didn't know what to do with it, Rooster. When she turned up dead, I knew they were after the tape. And now I've got it."

"You've looked at it?"

"Just the start," Beth said. "I'm in it. I knew what it was."

"It's in the machine now," Ray said, motioning toward the television with his empty bottle. "Beth would prefer not to be present when you watch it."

Beth stood up without looking once at me. She hugged Ray and disappeared into the other room, closing the door. I thought she looked a little better than when she'd first begun. I didn't have a mirror handy to see how I was taking it.

"You've been over this with her, Ray?"

"A dozen times."

"She has to go to the police. We can set up Felker—"

"I know, but you'd better wait. Beth didn't let me see the tape till late last night. I think you'd better look at it."

"Where are the holes?" I wanted to know. "Beth left Kathleen with Warman and Kathleen was dead the next morning. The tape is something Warman wanted. Kathleen was blackmailing him into selling her paintings."

"Wait," Ray insisted. "You're only hearing what you want to hear. Beth is a witness to the fact that *everyone* left the party. She was the last person there. She didn't see Rosalinda and Warman leave because she was in the kitchen with Kathleen."

"He was upstairs!" I nearly shouted.

"Warman and Rosalinda went by the Savoy on their way home, Rooster. A waiter, a bartender, three tables of people who know them saw them there. Rosalinda and Warman have an alibi."

"How long does it take to shoot a person?"

"You're still not listening, pal. Beth said it was a little after one when she got home. She lives ten minutes away if you walk it on your hands. Warman and Rosalinda were together at the Savoy a little after midnight. It's a tight alibi. Beth saw Kathleen alive well after that."

"Okay, he came back later."

"You're pushing it. You'd better see the tape, Rooster."

"Okay, I'll look at the damn tape." I knew I'd seen others like it. People who could afford video cameras had been taping the sexual act in all its varieties since the day the first cassette recorder was sold.

The tape was edited into two vignettes.

The initial scene was of Rosalinda standing, fully clothed, in a motel room. I hadn't expected this. The camera was stationary and apparently turned on by one of the performers, Rosalinda or Kathleen Kelly. Kathleen entered the view already in the buff. It was the first time I'd seen her alive.

She had an ample rear and rounded, pendulous breasts, though her body was that of a youth with a smooth unbroken complexion from head to toes. It was Rosalinda's face, however, that captured my attention. Her crystal blue eyes were focused into the distance as Kathleen approached, her hands touching Rosalinda. The audio was the sound of feet shuffling, breathing, a car honking outside, and a radio tuned to an easy-listening station.

Kathleen undressed Rosalinda. She made pleasant humming sounds as she removed items of Rosalinda's clothing. Rosalinda allowed her to. I was hoping for an earthquake to have interrupted the shoot. Kathleen's hands briefly caressed the other woman's flesh as it was exposed to the camera. Rosalinda closed her eyes.

A song ended on the radio, replaced by an Alka-Seltzer commercial. I might have laughed, but it was laugh racked by nerves on edge.

Rosalinda was blushing, holding steady as Kathleen kissed her body, moistened the skin around her navel, and removed Rosalinda's panties. Kathleen dropped to her knees. Rosalinda finally spoke. She told Kathleen to turn off the recorder.

I remembered the first time we'd made love, how Rosalinda had coaxed herself until the final moment. I didn't think she was going through with it. Then she took control and enjoyed it, wanted it, kept wanting it. We made love through the months of our relationship openly and without reservation. Still, it was the shy, coy Rosalinda I remembered best. That was the Rosalinda I loved the most. As I loved her now.

Kathleen stood, giggling, her back to the camera, blocking Rosalinda from view. Then she disappeared from the frame, leaving the woman of my life standing nude with her hands on her hips, a look of determined resolve having replaced the blush on her face. "Turn it off," Rosalinda said again, adamant, her glare burning holes in the videotape.

The screen went blank, filled with the patterned static of unused videotape. The moments wore on like a record stuck between the words of a lyric.

"Still with the living?" Ray asked as the moments turned into minutes. "There's more."

Sixteen

The static on the screen was replaced by a close-up of Rosalinda, a head shot.

She wore heavy makeup. Her lips were thickly coated with a deep red lipstick. She put on bedroom eyes, lowering her shadowed lids, feigning Marilyn Monroe perhaps. She pushed the point of her tongue over the white edges of her teeth then silently mouthed a carnal invitation to the viewer. Music playing in the background masked out the natural audio.

A tight edit switched scenes instantly. Rosalinda was tied to the bed in the bedroom on Fairmount Street. She was on her back, all four limbs outstretched. Beth and Kathleen took turns working the camera and making love to Rosalinda. Though tied in place, Rosalinda was an avid and generous participant.

I attempted to ignore the details, particularly the words breaking through the soundtrack, the voices of all three women vulgarly describing what they were doing and what they wanted to do next. The bruises on Rosalinda's wrists I'd recalled from our own recent tryst might not have been the scars of an attempted suicide. She bucked.

"Haven't we seen enough?" I said.

Ray turned off the television and punched the rewind button on the player. I struggled to gather my desperate thoughts.

"It was a birthday present for Warman," Ray informed me. "He'd been trying to get Rosalinda to do a three-way. He'd been grooming Kathleen as their potential playmate."

"Bringing her along," I said. "And she was getting a gallery contract out of the deal."

"Something like that, Rooster. The house was part of the setup. I think he was sneaking Kathleen into their lives sideways. Rosalinda came around. According to Beth, Rosalinda showed up on Kathleen's doorstep with the suggestion they make a tape for Warman's birthday."

"It doesn't sound like Rosalinda." But it sure did look like her.

"Kathleen was a strong personality. She dominated Beth for a time. But Beth was breaking away. I'm helping her now."

"What about Rosalinda? What was she getting in return from him? What was she getting out of the relationship, Ray? I just don't understand it."

"Money," Ray suggested, but he didn't push it. "The rest of the story is a couple months ago Rosalinda threw Warman a birthday bash at their house on Ward Parkway. All the important artsy people were there. And Kathleen."

"Am I going to want to hear this?"

"No. Anyway, Rosalinda takes the birthday boy into the master bedroom and gives him the tape. He watches it while the party goes on, then joins the crowd. The tape was his present, a promise of things to come."

"He's not in the tape. He wouldn't need to kill someone over it. It's not the tape, Ray."

"Later, as the birthday party's winding down, Rosalinda hides Kathleen in the bedroom closet."

"Was Beth there?"

"She wasn't, but Kathleen told her about it afterwards. So, Warman and Rosalinda call it a night, go to bed, and Kathleen slithers out of the closet to join them."

"A smashing success," I snarled.

"This tape is a copy, Rooster. Kathleen made a copy."

"Blackmail?" I considered my own question.

"You tell me," Ray said. "According to Beth, neither Rosalinda nor Warman knew the copy existed. But Kathleen could have told them. Under any circumstances, it looks as if she was getting what she wanted. Warman eventually sold one of her paintings for relatively big numbers."

"It's the only copy now. You can bet your sweet ass, Ray, that Warman destroyed his when Kathleen was murdered."

"It follows," Ray allowed.

"Dammit, Ray, the tape explains the bombing. Warman couldn't find the tape, so he had the house burned down. But he'd have to know she'd copied it. Maybe he started to back out of their deal to make Kathleen rich and famous. She pulls out her ace in the hole and tells him she has a copy of the birthday video."

"Like you said, Rooster, it doesn't incriminate him."

"Maybe not directly. But in the eyes of the police, the video might be seen as motive for his killing Kathleen Kelly. It was his wife. Besides, don't those Mayflower descendants give a big hairy crap about their reputations in the community and all like that?"

"I want the bastard nailed, Rooster."

Hearing it from Ray surprised me.

"What he did to Beth mean something to you?"

"Sure it does," Ray confessed. "Women," he added. "What're you going to do? You can't live with 'em and it's against the law to shoot 'em."

I smiled broadly in spite of everything. "At least we can hope it still is."

Ray offered to make me a copy of the tape before turning it over to Lieutenant Felker. I impolitely declined the offer. I never wanted to see the thing again. I told Ray about the Polaroids and the erotic portrait of Rosalinda I'd recovered from Inside Moves.

"It might not have meant much before, but after the murder it ties Warman to Kathleen. So he had the gallery bombed to destroy the painting and the pictures of Rosalinda. That would explain both bombings, Rooster."

"All the paintings were there, Ray. All her work. For all I know, there might have been several of Rosalinda. No matter, he managed to destroy the connection between himself and the dead girl, or so he thinks. And, at the same time, he makes it appear to the police as if he's being persecuted."

"At least he thought the stuff would be destroyed. I'm telling you, Rooster, either someone knows what you've got or at least they're afraid of what you might have."

"So, you think he killed her, Ray?"

"Looks like, ol' buddy."

I should have told him about the stamps. But Ray might have told Beth. And I didn't want that information to spill out during her chat with the Metropolitan Squad. The lurid artwork, the Polaroids, even the videotape were one thing. The error stamps were quite another. Somebody was looking to make a killing.

I thought of Bodyguard as a showerhead.

Walking around the Crown Center fountains that were embedded in the sidewalk, the lug grinned when a fine spray caught in the breeze dusted our faces. There were spaces between the upper teeth on one side of Bodyguard's mouth you could stick your fingers through. I pictured water pumping out the holes in his mouth and children dancing circles around him this summer. If Bodyguard would hold still for it, he'd have made a capable fountain.

Bodyguard uttered not a single syllable until we pulled into the driveway of Lips's house on Charlotte. "They get by me, you better run like hell," he advised.

I wasn't certain who *they* were, but anyone who could get by Bodyguard positively merited running away from.

My knee caught as I tumbled out of the biker's pickup and I nearly fell. The knee grew stiff when left in one position too long and, though constantly sore, it hurt like new to work out the stiffness. Of course, I could run if I had to. The thought of it didn't make me smile.

The shed was a small metal building inside the backyard privacy fence. Bodyguard kept his distance while I placed the key into the padlock. I doubted he stood back so far to protect our rear, but I couldn't blame him for being afraid of bombs.

As I slid the metal door along its track, I said, "The guy with the bombs was assassinated in his motel room."

"Some bombs don't go off till you touch 'em," Bodyguard said. "They rig up a gun that fires in your face when you open the door."

Wired guns were more a homespun technique, an indiscriminate guard against intrusion. Warman wasn't out to kill just anybody. Bodyguard came forward.

"These ones?" He pointed at the two cardboard boxes of paperwork set in front of the lawn mower. I removed what I wanted, an envelope that was sitting on top. Bodyguard stacked the cartons and carried them to the truck.

"Put them inside the cab," I called after him, closing the shed. I left the padlock open in case Metro had given me the only key. Remembering the gun, I searched the mailbox for the key to the house. It was right where Ray had told me it would be.

But the front door was unlocked. The last time this happened to me, there was a dead girl upstairs. Bodyguard watched the street for the approach of bad guys. A man who would hire a bomb might not care who he killed. I convinced myself I was being paranoid and opened the door. Inside, the blinds were closed. The house was dark.

Bodyguard cautiously approached the porch, while I found my way into the living room. Holding the manila envelope with the Polaroids of Rosalinda in one hand, I felt between the couch cushions with the other. The moment my hand touched the gun, a frigid chill sped up my spine and back down again as I saw something from the corner of my eye.

Danny lay on his back in the middle of the floor.

Bodyguard stepped inside the house in time to hear me gasp. I found the light switch and, upon a closer look, made my way to the table at the end of the couch to use the phone. I dialed 911, the gun clenched tightly in my hand. Bodyguard bent down beside Danny's outstretched body.

"Don't bring him around," I ordered. "He's out from pain."

Danny's boyish face, though darkly bruised in one spot, was as pale as ivory. His hands, however, were a bright reddish purple. Swollen fat with blood, they hung limp at the ends of his arms, looking like stub-fingered balloons. The bones in his wrists were shattered.

"One at a time," Bodyguard said. "They wanted him to tell them something."

"Something he didn't know," I said.

Then the emergency operator was on the line. He connected me with ambulance dispatch and I told them to bring a hypo with something in it for pain. Then I called the emergency room at the KU medical center to let them know what was coming in so they could be prepared.

"Who?" I shouted at Bodyguard as I slammed down the phone. "The Black Angels? The Sundowners? Dammit, Bodyguard, tell me who did this!"

"Meza doesn't know," Bodyguard said, his loyalty apparent. "He don't take the job, it goes to anybody."

"He's bleeding to death," I pleaded. "Right now as we speak. Who did it? Somebody knows who did it!"

Bodyguard stood up from Danny's side, shaking his head slowly in what could have been a gesture of sympathy. "Somebody meaner than me," he said.

I quieted. "You know what that smell is? You *know* what that is?" I asked. "He shit his pants. It hurt that bad, Bodyguard. He was that scared. . . ."

"Scared ain't nothin' death won't cure," Bodyguard drawled.

I dropped to my knees next to Danny. Laying aside the .38 caliber revolver, I gently picked up his head, turning it sideways to make certain he wasn't strangling on his own vomit. Danny's breathing was labored. My knee didn't hurt a bit.

"If I hired you, would you kill somebody?" I asked my towering comrade.

"I work for Meza," Bodyguard said, as if that explained everything. It did.

Rosalinda in the buff watched dispassionately from inside the portrait Lips had placed on the mantel. Her pose contributed greatly to the malevolent ambiance of the room. I could never make myself like that painting. Rosalinda had done this to Danny by placing her splayed fingertips just so.

Seventeen

A wind moved into town.

I stood in darkness outside the emergency room, watching a man smoke a cigarette. He leaned against the railing that protected the heliport, an expanse of pavement with a large white cross painted in its center. The lighted tip of cigarette glowed bright red in the wind. Stray embers lifted and fell on the breeze, disappeared like meteorites or shooting stars.

It turned out Danny had been at the house all the time, sleeping off a severe hangover after calling in sick. Now, he'd miss a few more days of work at least and learn to write his name without moving his wrist. I held the manila envelope of dirty pictures, my gun hidden inside my jacket. I'd instructed Bodyguard to see that word got out the job was done. There was nothing left to look for.

I wished something would show up I could shoot at. A careening carload of comic-book machine-gun mobsters would do just fine. I needed something to strike out against, something to take a swing at. A green Crown Victoria is a stupid car. You see one of those in your neighborhood, you have my permission to punch out the driver.

Warman existed in shadow, somewhere out of the wind, a prey inside the shelter of thorns and bramble bush.

Perhaps the only way to conquer demons is to march right into the lava pit, your heart held high in one hand, and kick their teeth out. I could go to Warman's house and break all his windows with hurled dirt clods and rocks. Or, hell, I could look for Marc Morelli myself. Maybe he was waiting for me.

I could've said something nasty and mean to the man flipping his burning cigarette in a high arch onto the heliport. He might want to make something of it.

Metro appeared at my side. The surgeon would call his office in about a half hour with a prognosis.

"Let's go call Lips," I said. "You got a tape player that'll take a minicassette?"

If I could see Warman's face again, I'd know why he killed Kathleen Kelly. His motive was at the vague edges of my thoughts. I only needed to bring it into view. Like a word you've forgotten only at the instant you need to use it.

We crossed a parking lot and wound up in a quadrangle formed by four brick-and-concrete buildings. Metro slipped a plastic card into a metal box that unlocked the courtyard entry to the administration building. He used a key, once inside the elevator, to unlock the third floor. A pleasant-faced black housekeeper Metro knew by name smiled and said hello. He introduced her to me, saying that she always took good care of him.

"He works more late nights than the president," she said, obviously proud of her third-floor dedicated civil servant. "And weekends sometimes, too."

Especially during football season, I thought. Truth was, Metro lived alone in a one-bedroom apartment on the Kansas side. I'd visited it once and had been put off by the dismal home life of my friend. There wasn't a plant or a pet to be seen. Metro kept his bookmaking paperwork hidden in his locked desk at work. He took afternoon naps on a couch in the back room. The office and the neighborhood bars were Metro's real home. His apartment was nothing more than a place to sleep, a place to spend the night once the bars closed.

I wished I had one.

Metro's office was standard state university fare with horribly old paneling. The black-and-red swirl carpeting had been in poor taste when it was bought on low bid twenty-five years ago. The metal bookcase was decorated with a number of sports trophies that gleamed in the harsh overhead lighting. Metro coached the med center's co-ed softball team in city competition each summer. Win or lose, each player received the same trophy. This was because Metro bought them himself.

I wished I had one.

Metro turned on the coffee maker. I wanted one of those, too.

"I'd just fixed up a pot when I got your call from the ER. I didn't know how long I was going to be here. You say you've got a tape worth hearing?"

"It won't make the top forty," I said.

I tossed the envelope of Polaroids onto Metro's desk while he popped the cassette into the hand-size player.

There were three calls on the wiretap. The first was Rosalinda confirming hotel reservations at the Chase Park in St. Louis for Thursday. The overly polite clerk not only confirmed the reservation, but gave Rosalinda the room number.

I stopped the tape. It was more than hearing her voice that set me back.

"How far is Omaha?" I asked. "In minutes."

"Four hours top," Metro said. "Divided interstate all the way there and all the way back."

"She pulled a turnaround, Metro. Flew there, then drove back." He didn't know what I was talking about.

According to the itinerary Felker had, Rosalinda was in

Omaha through Thursday morning for a dealer-to-dealer antique show. Then she flew to Des Moines for an art auction. I wondered if Warman had arranged the false itinerary to keep me from contacting her. Or maybe he thought I'd drive to Omaha to catch up with her and Warman would be free to go about his piratical business.

"When?" Metro wanted to know.

"Maybe she's driving back right now. Maybe she's already here."

"Here? The med center?"

I played the remainder of the tape. Next up was my impersonation of a drunk ordering a pizza. The last call came in after two o'clock in the morning, give or take five minutes. Warman answered the phone.

"It's done," a male voice told him. "When do I get my fee?"

"Name a time and place," Warman said.

"As soon as possible. I'm booking my butt out of this town."

The caller gave him a room number at a hotel near the airport. The voice belonged to Marty Ryan. That much and much more was evident. I had Warman by the balls.

No wonder he was so upset when he'd discovered his phone had been tapped. Even now, he must be running scared. Ruddick had managed to tape a conversation between a dead man and the man who killed him, between a professional arsonist and his client.

"We've got to cover our behinds," I said, letting out a low whistle. "What happened to Danny is a mild inconvenience compared to what this man would do if he knew we had this tape."

Metro was duly impressed when I explained the significance of the recording.

"What do you mean *we*, paleface?" he asked.

·   ·   ·

We were on our third cups of coffee when Metro got the call.

"Doc says Danny won't be hanging drywall for quite some time," he said, hanging up the phone.

"Whatever that's supposed to mean."

"Physician's humor," Metro said. "They all stay up late watching M*A*S*H reruns. The prognosis is good. There's no nerve damage. But he wanted to know how it happened."

I telephoned Lips at the number Ray had given me.

"They won't be bringing him around till tomorrow afternoon," I said, when she insisted on coming to the hospital. "The surgery's going to take a few hours. They have to do some vascular repair."

"Will he be able to use his hands?"

"About six months of piano lessons and they should be as good as new," I assured her. I urged Lips to go ahead and spend the night with her coworker, while simultaneously attempting to convince her the danger was over.

"I feel responsible, Rooster. After Ray called me at work, I phoned the house. But all I got was my answering machine. I figured he'd gone on to work."

If anyone felt responsible it was me.

"They were after the stuff I brought over last night," I said. "Metro put it in the shed and put a lock on it. Danny had no idea it was there."

"Who, Rooster? Who did it?"

"We're going to find out, Lips. Hired hands is all I know."

"Isn't there something we can do to them?"

"I've been thinking about that," I confessed.

"I'd like to hurt them real bad," Lips said slowly, purposefully. "Real damn bad, Rooster."

"I have an idea who hired them."

"What about the stuff you have? Won't those guys come after you?"

"It's been destroyed. We're putting the word out."

"The painting?"

"It wasn't the painting they were after. It's still on your mantel."

"You know what, Rooster? I don't think I want it there anymore."

Metro wanted to know what we did next once I was off the line. I had an idea we should pick up the painting. I removed the photocopies of the error stamps from the envelope containing the Polaroids of Rosalinda. I pocketed them, folded. I securely taped the envelope shut while Metro went to the rest room to rinse the coffee pot. The Polaroids weren't needed now that the video of Rosalinda was on its way to Lieutenant Felker.

The photocopied stamps, however, were priceless. I planned to somehow, somewhere and soon wave them under Warman's nose.

On our way out, I trailed the cord to the vacuum cleaner whirring away in another office. The older housekeeper reminded me of everyone's cheerful grandma. I hadn't had one. Metro gave her the thick manila envelope once she'd shut down the vacuum.

"You want me to drop this by the mail room on my dinner break?" she asked Metro.

Something clicked. I stared at her. You'd have to ask the housekeeper whether my mouth dropped open, whether my hair stood on end. It may have.

"Can you see it gets into the incinerator without anyone looking at it?" Metro requested.

"You know you can trust me, honey," she said, accepting the assignment. I was still staring. Something she'd said. Something Beth had said. It came together and I knew the motive for Kathleen Kelly's murder. It was a cold reason for murder and had very little to do with the passions of the young artist.

The black housekeeper looked at me like I needed slapped. Metro tugged me away from my frozen pose, dragged me by the sleeve out the office door into the hallway.

"Thanks!" I called to her. "I love you!" But she'd already turned the vacuum cleaner back on.

On our way across seventeen different parking lots to the rented Camaro, I went over it again in silence, oblivious to the night, the wind. My sore left knee came right along. The videotape opened up Warman's secret private life like a can of exploding worms. He had used his money and his position to influence Rosalinda, to change her. I wasn't being naive. The change happened to some people who tasted money for the first time, real money, lots of money. Her behavior would have shocked me had I been a younger man in love, but I didn't blame Rosalinda.

She was the victim. She'd come under the control of a demon, a two-legged demon driving a Mercedes convertible.

But Warman's control hadn't extended to Kathleen Kelly. She'd plainly been a stronger young woman than Warman was accustomed to meeting. Kathleen Kelly had been murdered because she had not been captured by Warman's spell. The specific motive was my new idea. The photos, the painting, the videotape were direct connections between Warman and Kathleen; they were not, though, the reason she'd been murdered.

Once she'd been snuffed, it was worth burning her house to cover up evidence. Once she'd been snuffed, it was worth bombing the gallery to destroy her paintings and any other menacing secrets that could be tossed into the fire. Then Warman killed the arsonist. It was his years in the CIA, I was convinced. Even if he'd only pushed pens and filed folders, he had associated with people who routinely used murder to accomplish their goals.

I had a feather in my shorts to check out the motive. I drove to Crown Center. In the covered parking lot, Metro put his hand on my arm. I needed to stretch my left knee, but I waited.

"About that green LTD, Rooster." he said.

"Morelli?"

"One of his second bananas. He was in Jack's while you were there Monday. I didn't know what to say."

"He's the one who's been talking to you about joining the club?"

"Yeah, pal. Like I said, I may quit altogether. Since Marc got out, all the small fry are being gobbled up. I have to lay off my bets with somebody. Shit, man, I don't know."

"What's his name?"

"Get this, Rooster. He goes by *Moe*. As in *Larry, Curly, and*."

"That's it?" The bastard went into the house on Fairmount Street while I squirreled around at the grocery store. He'd followed me there from Jack's. He'd found the body, waited till I got back, and hightailed it to call the cops.

"That and he's one mean son of a bitch, Rooster. He's got dead eyes, you know what I mean? He looks at you and there's nothing for you to look back at. Moe doesn't give the impression he screws up a lot."

He'd left the door to Kathleen Kelly's house unlocked.

"Maybe Rosalinda and I will leave town before he shows up again," I said.

"I get the strong impression, Rooster, he's just watching the show. Word is Marc Morelli would like to talk to you in person. I probably shouldn't say this, but there's a, uh, reward for bringing you to him."

"Worth your while?"

"Hey, Rooster! I'll put you two together the minute you tell me you're ready to kill that prick."

"I don't have to, Metro. You understand? I don't *have to*."

"You do if you want to live in this town, brother. And that's the truth."

I popped the door, sat there a moment, then tried to

smile. "I've been thinking about St. Louis lately. Hear that river is one hell of a view."

Ray let us in. Beth, wearing the same dress, sat on the couch, her feet tucked up. The television was on.

"Why don't you guys go downstairs and split a pitcher of beer," I suggested. "I need to talk to Beth."

Eighteen

I attempted a comforting smile. It didn't work.

I turned down the sound of the television. She started talking as soon as I had my back turned.

"The Metropolitan Squad detective came by and looked at the tape," Beth said. "Things will be all right now. He took it with him."

"That's good." I sat down on the couch next to her, but not too close. "It's about time you go home now, isn't it?"

"I don't feel safe yet." She watched the silent TV.

"I'm the one Warman's after now. You're in no danger."

"But Danny . . . Ray told me what happened to him."

"It's a whole new game, Beth. It's just me and Warman looking for a time and a place to meet."

"I'm sorry, Rooster. I got you into all of this. I knew how you felt about Rosalinda. I could have said something."

"You did say something, Beth. I just wasn't listening."

"About doll eyes? Yeah, you got that wrong. I was talking about you, and you thought I meant Rosalinda."

That wasn't the something I had in mind.

Beth leaned her head against the cushions and closed her

eyes briefly. I took her hand and squeezed it. She held my palm for a moment, then released it. For some reason, Beth was about to cry.

"Kathleen," I began, "she was killed because of something she knew."

"She was blackmailing Warman?"

"Maybe. But not with the videotape."

"What then?"

"Two things. The night of the party at Kathleen's house. And Warman's birthday party."

Beth sighed heavily. She knitted her fingers, intent on helping. She told me, or seemed to, all she knew. We went over what Kathleen had told her about hiding in the bedroom closet the night Rosalinda gave Warman the birthday video, about having sex with the married couple.

And we went over again the things Kathleen had said to Beth on the front porch the night of her celebration party on Fairmount Street.

"If what I think is correct, whatever was going on between Kathleen and Warman hit the fan the night of *her* party. But it had begun much earlier, Beth."

"She was so upset, Rooster. Throwing everyone out. She was having a fit. I didn't know what was happening."

"I want you to think back, Beth. Kathleen talked about the mailbox, how it would make her rich."

"I guess someone was going to send her money."

"That's what I thought at first. Please think this over carefully. Did Kathleen mention anything to you about postage stamps?"

Beth watched Vanna White turn three P's in a four-word puzzle. Then she shook her head.

"Just the mail, Rooster. She just said the mail was going to make her rich."

"That's fine," I said, wanting to encourage her.

"I'm sorry."

"It's okay, Beth. Really. Now, Kathleen told you about

Warman's birthday party. That she'd hidden in the bedroom closet. And when Warman came to bed she and Rosalinda joined him."

"Yes?"

"Did Kathleen tell you anything about what went on while she was in the closet."

"Only that she was there a long time, waiting."

"Waiting for what?"

"Waiting for them to be ready for her."

"Rosalinda *and* Warman?"

"I guess so. No, wait," Beth said, pausing. "Just Rosalinda. Warman came to bed, but she had to wait for Rosalinda. Kathleen said she was afraid he would open the closet and ruin the surprise."

"That's it," I whispered.

"Wait a second, Rooster," Beth said, snapping her mental fingers. "You're right. It wasn't the night of the party at her house, but Kathleen did say something about a stamp."

"Yes?"

"She asked me if I had any idea what a one-dollar stamp was worth. I thought it was a philosophical question or something."

I nearly jumped off the couch.

"And this was after the birthday party for Warman and before her party?"

"Uh-huh," Beth said, unsure she followed what I was after.

I stood up too quickly, snagging the pain in my knee. I paced to walk it out. "Picture this, Beth. Warman's having a party. He doesn't have a chance to be alone for long. It's his party. He can't just disappear, right?"

Beth nodded.

"Early on, he previews the videotape. Then he rejoins the party. He's stuck until the last guests leave. Finally, he's alone. Rosalinda is emptying ashtrays or rinsing glasses. For whatever reason she doesn't come right to bed. He goes into the bedroom and then what?"

"He takes off his clothes and goes to bed?"

"He makes a phone call, Beth! Or he takes a phone call. Either way, Kathleen's in the closet and she hears something she isn't supposed to. *Then* Rosalinda comes to bed and we know what happens next."

I stopped. I looked at Beth. I looked away.

"I'm convinced," I said, "that Kathleen Kelly overheard Warman discussing a deal to buy the invert errors."

"Invert errors?"

"That's what she meant by asking the worth of a dollar stamp," I said, talking to myself. That's exactly what she meant.

"I don't understand, Rooster."

"Kathleen overheard an illegal deal taking place. It was big money, Beth, that's the gist of it."

I began pacing again. Warman could have spent five years slowly feeding the stamps into the marketplace for his client. Yet, one extraneous person knowing so many of the stamps existed could turn the entire enterprise into a huge loss. Kathleen was that person.

"So he kills her?"

"It takes a while, Beth. Maybe he's not sure she knows anything. But he worries about it. He asks Rosalinda about it. Eventually, he realizes Kathleen did overhear him. But he still doesn't know whether she's a threat."

"And then he kills her?"

"I think Kathleen pushed him. She put two and two together and pushed him. That's what was going on upstairs at her party the night she was murdered. Warman was making a last effort to placate Kathleen and still make a fortune."

"That's why she said she was going to be rich," Beth added for me.

"But she was also upset. She didn't trust him. Obviously

for good reason. Kathleen Kelly pushed Warman and Warman pushed back.''

"Maybe I'd better stay here a couple more weeks.''

Wheel of Fortune, spinning on the television, had slots for Lose a Turn and Bankrupt. The colorful wheel should also have spaces for disillusionment, terror, despair, and murder. Permanent maiming and fatal disease. Were the Wheel of Fortune the wheel of life, you'd have to think twice before taking a free spin. And make Vanna wipe that smile off her face.

"I've got to run, Beth. Ray will keep you posted.''

"There's something I want to tell you first. It's important to me that you know.''

"Go ahead.''

"Well, don't stand by the door, dammit. Come over here.''

I did.

"I'm not a lesbian, Rooster.''

"Okay.'' Our eyes locked. I tried not to look uncomfortable. I hate personal confessions. I really do. They're none of my business.

"I don't know if this happens to guys. It's that, well, for a time I was all alone. And Kathleen was such a strong and exciting person.''

Was I supposed to say something here? Probably not.

"That's part of it, Rooster. The rest is she was in love with me. She really was.''

"It's easy to see how that could happen,'' I said, trying a compliment.

"I didn't want to hurt anyone,'' Beth weakly claimed, as if she'd failed.

"You didn't, Beth. If it didn't hurt you. Are you pulling through?''

"Yeah,'' she said, her eyes wet. "Yeah, yeah, yeah. . . . go on, get out of here!''

. . .

"If anyone's following me, I want to talk to them."

"Don't expect me to point 'em out for you, Rooster. I'd just as soon get a good night's sleep."

"Hungry?"

"Always."

"I have an idea for supper, once we're through."

"I don't like the sound of that."

"Wine and cheese, Metro. You'll love it."

I dropped him off at the 7-Eleven on Thirty-ninth Street, then returned to my motel room across the street from KU Med, to my duffel bag, dirty clothes, and a dead fly on the carpet next to the dresser.

Metro answered the pay telephone outside the convenience store with a growly and disgruntled "Yeah?"

"We're this close, pal," I said into the wiretapped receiver.

"The stamps?" Metro asked, as he'd been coached on the ride over. "And don't call me pal, Mac," he added, improvising.

"Hey, now, we're partners," I consoled. "Of course *the stamps.*"

"How many?"

"They're all on the line."

"Three sheets?"

"Yes sir, yes sir, three sheets full," I sang, playing the hustling jerk. "Worth coming to town for, don't you think?"

"You see 'em?"

"Good as. Just be sure you have the money."

"What's the numbers?" Metro was throwing himself into the role. I was afraid he'd start haggling over the phone.

"Bargain basement," I promised. "I'll be in touch tomorrow. Same phone?"

"Why not," Metro grumbled. "Same time, too. Just don't make me wait, Mac."

"Got you," I said, hanging up. I was talking to Warman. I had his balls, I might as well twist them. The tape of this call would not only be enough to drive him crazy, as Ray and I had calculated. It should also be enough off-center information to have Ray's dad asking his new client a few sharp questions.

As Metro hiked the dark block and a half to the motel I gave the murder of Kathleen Kelly further thought. It somehow made sense in this upside-down world that people would kill each other over a printing error. Now if I could just get Rosalinda right side up. . . .

I stepped outside the confines of the motel room to test the weather and to see if who I expected might be parked there. My jacket felt comfortably snug as the cold September wind ruffled my hair. A sweater under would have been more comfortable. So would a flannel shirt. A bullet-proof vest.

The unmarked Dodge was pulled up alongside the chain-link fence that surrounds the motel swimming pool. I didn't like this guy, but I had a message for him. I walked to the car. I was smart enough to leave the .38 in the room.

I tapped on the hood, came around to the passenger side, and waited. The young officer in the car wore a jersey sweater and was chewing gum. He leaned across the seat and unlocked the door. I climbed in.

"How's it going, Officer? Anything I can do for you?"

"You have something to say, Franklin, say it." The plainclothes police officer stared at me with his best poker face. It wasn't much. I turned off the chirping radio scan.

"They tell you I shoot people in the head?"

The officer didn't respond. I worked to stay calm. I wanted to get this right.

"You must be new, to draw an assignment like this," I went on. "You got a union card, though, don't you?"

The car had municipal KCK plates. The officer smacked his gum in reply.

"You know your business manager, don't you? Danny Harrison? A fine man. He's a local boy, you know."

Again, no response.

"You from around here?"

The cop stared blank-faced at the windshield. But he chewed his gum more slowly now.

"Some guys busted his hands today. He's across the street in surgery right now." I fought not to speak too rapidly, fought not to shout. "They came right into the house and put his arms, one at a time, over the edge of a chair leg and then stomped his hands. Until his wrists popped. You ever hear anything like that?"

"What do you want, Franklin?"

"Hurt so bad, he shit his pants. Passed out and his hands filled up with blood. Someone hadn't found him, his whole arms would have swelled up until he looked like Popeye on a spinach overdose."

The cop stopped chewing his gum.

"I want your boss to know something. You work for Muro, don't you?"

A slight movement of his head might have been taken for a nod.

"You know what Muro would like to know? He's a good man, Muro, and he'd probably like to know that off-duty police officers had set up your business manager. Muro, he probably wouldn't tolerate that sort of horseshit from his officers, you think?"

I wished I hadn't quit smoking. This would have been a great time to burn a hole in the upholstery.

"Two KCK officers got off shift this morning, uniform guys, and followed a friend of mine to the house where Danny Harrison was staying. Then they reported back to somebody who came around and busted Danny's hands. The cops were free-lancing, you know what I mean?

"Hard to believe cops would do that, Officer. You could probably find out who those two guys are, don't you think? Got off work this morning, have this four-wheel-drive pickup. Ate some pie at Shoney's then set up *your* business manager. That would really piss me off if I were Muro."

It was hard to stay angry with this kid sitting behind the wheel. I hadn't expected the KCK detective would be so young. Maybe it was a good sign. Maybe the guy was clean.

"Those two officers wouldn't be men a person could trust, I'd bet. Muro wouldn't mind knowing who they were. Hey, you'd probably like to know who you could trust, too, wouldn't you? Yeah, I would."

That was about it.

"It's up to you," I told the kid. "I know it would eat at me if people I worked with were doing this kind of thing. Maybe I'd just spread the word with the other guys. That might be enough. But, I tell you the truth, I would do something."

I pulled myself up out of the seat and gave the door a healthy close. I walked slowly off on my sore knee.

Talking to the junior detective had been better than professional therapy. One of those silent guys should always be around in their Dodge when you need them. Metro was coming up the sidewalk, nodding his head frantically to direct my attention to something behind me.

I nearly dropped. Instead, I turned and saw, beyond the Dodge, a dark blue Cadillac. As I looked at it, the Cadillac started up and drove hastily away. I noticed the gold-colored trim on the sedan, but couldn't see a thing inside of it.

Metro reached me and put a hand on my shoulder.

"Everything go okay?"

"It all depends on how long it takes Ray's dad to get the recording to Warman," I said. "I tell you one thing, Metro. It won't take Warman long to come looking for us once he hears it."

"Why do you keep saying *us?*" Metro demanded to know.

In the driveway, Metro kept the Camaro running, the windows rolled up, while I went into Lips's house. I'd dropped in to turn on a few lights. On the way out, I grabbed Kathleen Kelly's portrait of Rosalinda. I got the thing into what was supposed to be a backseat and climbed into the car. Metro had the heater on.

And the radio. "Three to nothing, second inning," he announced. "Guess who?"

"The Royals," I said. "And I'm not guessing."

"You're not guessing, all right." Metro put the car into reverse. "You're dreaming."

On our way back to State Line, Metro drove through Westport. There was an empty space in the block where Inside Moves had been, a stretch of orange plastic netting along the sidewalk. In heaven or hell, Marty Ryan could be proud of his work. People on the street ignored the site of last night's destruction.

"I'm worried about you, Metro. All you think about is sports and point spreads. You need more exposure to culture."

"Whose culture?" he asked, offended.

"The arts, pal. The arts!"

"You sure they don't mind if you eat the food? I mean, you don't have to buy something in order to eat?"

"They only get upset when nobody comes by to eat anything," I said.

"Okay, then," Metro said, looking for a place to park. "It's just that I've never been to one of these before."

"Don't worry about it. No one's going to ask you what the art means or anything like that."

"You say that now, Rooster. But I'm the one who has to come up with the bullshit if they do."

"Small price to pay for supper, huh?"

I looked for a particular color of Mercedes convertible parked nearby. It was possible Warman would attend the first-Wednesday exhibits of competing galleries.

Meg McNally, the tile artist, chatted nervously with a large, thinly bearded man. Her boyfriend, I thought. Metro kept close to me as I studied Meg's finished and mounted porcelain tiles. Pigs and cows, just as she'd promised. One series of five tiles were vignettes of a cow jumping over the moon. As the cow's flight progressed from tile to tile, the phases of the moon progressed. At the apex of the bovine's lunar leap, the moon was completely full.

"Who knows, Metro, maybe one day you'll give painting a try."

"Yeah, Rooster. And maybe one day you'll pitch the home opener for the New York Yankees."

Meg wore pleated charcoal pants that tapered to the ankle, a red silk blouse under an oversized gray shirt left open and with the sleeves rolled up. A necklace of strung ceramic pieces she'd likely made herself circled her throat. She put on her brightest smile as we approached.

"I'm Meg McNally," she announced, offering a firm handshake. "Did you enjoy my work?"

She was getting it down.

"How am I doing?" Meg asked in a smaller, more intimate voice.

I winked. I introduced Metro, and Meg introduced the bearded man who turned out to be one of the other artists whose work was on exhibit. Meg joined Metro and me as we made our way to the reception table.

"Do I have to sign the register to get something to eat?" Metro asked.

"Yes," Meg said, her green eyes brightening. "But if you're smart, you'll use a fake name. I always do."

A glass of wine in one hand, I surveyed the remainder of

the show with Meg. Metro stayed close to the crackers and cheese.

"Who did these?" I asked, referring to a number of wire sculptures of Harley-Davidson motorcycles, each extremely detailed and mounted with the front tire lifted high in the air.

"A guy named Feathers," she said. "He's Cherokee and the arts coalitions are always listing him as an American Indian artist. Nobody quite realizes he's heavy into motorcycles until he puts his show up. He belongs to a biker gang, the whole bit."

"That should teach people something about stereotypes. Is he here?"

"He never comes to his shows. Some of the bikers have been, though. They're a real hoot."

I grinned.

"One of them came in and sat in the middle of the floor," Meg continued. "He took out a joint and lit it and just stared at the Harleys like they were the real Madonna while everyone walked around him. Then he got up and left."

"Is the show going well for you?"

"I sold every piece on display in the first forty-five minutes." Meg said this as if she regretted it. "I'm either very popular or very cheap. They take so long to make it'll be six months before I can exhibit again."

"Not the worst scenario for a first show," I suggested.

"I was thinking maybe the stuff's *too* commercial."

"You don't want to starve forever," I said.

She giggled. "I guess I'm nervous is all. It seems so successful I figure there has to be a catch somewhere."

Meg slipped her hand in mine as we went to find Metro. I recognized her light perfume as Krizia and would have complimented her good taste, but I knew it would embarrass her. I retrieved the keys to the Camaro from my Creole bookmaker and told Meg I had something in the car to show her.

"Don't fall for it, sweetie," Metro warned her. Then requested that I check the score on the radio while I was out there.

Outside, Meg stopped me on the sidewalk. She took my hand again, held it lightly. My hand felt too big, too clumsy for a girl to hold.

"I'm not trying to say anything big," she began. "But there's a party after the show, about ten o'clock or so. And if you wanted to go, I—"

I squeezed her hand. It was about ten degrees warmer than a burning coal.

"I hate parties," I said, telling the truth. "If I were a little younger, though, I'd gladly put up with one for you."

Meg blushed. "I didn't mean that exactly," she stammered. "It's . . . well, I mean . . . it's like you're a friend or something, a close friend. Someone I used to know and like a long time ago. And we met only yesterday." Meg shrugged. "It's an odd feeling. I can't explain it, but I trust you somehow."

"You shouldn't," I said. I tugged gently on her hand, wrapped my arm around her shoulder, and walked her to the rental car. She made me feel tall. I'd married women for less.

Without fanfare, I gave the painting to her.

"Where'd you get this?" Meg asked, astonished. "I heard they were all destroyed. It was like Kathleen Kelly never existed. . . ."

"Is your car nearby?"

"Behind the gallery," Meg said. "Oh, I can't believe it. And I hadn't seen this one. It's very good, don't you think?"

Rosalinda was good, all right. She was very, very good.

"I can't tell you why, Meg, but you shouldn't show it to anyone for a while, a week or two anyway."

Meg held the painting close to her breast in both hands. She didn't ask me to explain. On our way back from tucking the painting into Meg's car, she stopped me on the sidewalk again.

"Can I ask you something silly?"

"If it's too silly, may I laugh?"

"No."

"Okay."

"Are you in love with someone?"

"The boy I once was," I finally, carefully said, "is in love with the idea of you."

Meg kissed me on the cheek. I embraced her, feeling the gentle dust of her breath on my ear. I hoped she didn't notice the bulge of the .38 tucked inside my waistband.

Rosalinda was my deeper excitement. The closer I came to nailing Warman, the closer I came to seeing Rosalinda again.

What might have been a broken tree trunk was propped against the brick wall of the gallery as Meg and I turned the corner.

Bodyguard. Of course, if this guy had been a tree, squirrels would have moved into holes in the ground centuries ago.

I figured he'd come with a message for me, but Bodyguard completely ignored my gesture of greeting as Meg and I approached the front door of the gallery. We left him and the other streetlights outside.

My reaction upon seeing Rick Meza was a mixture of anger and awe. The stocky, good-looking biker wore full club colors and a woman of considerable elegance on his arm. They'd shown up to demonstrate community support for Feathers's work, no doubt.

The slender, raven-haired beauty was taller than Meza. She wore expensive jewelry and a dress that appeared to be made of cream-and-butter-colored scarves. She also wore an aura of wealth, power, and connections. She was one of those few women who inherit a physical grace and ease that make them look entirely at home on Hepplewhite furniture.

Meza could have done something to save Danny Harrison from suffering his dreadful fate. That was the bottom line on which my anger stood, bubbled, grew. I hated Meza's thick hair, his white teeth, his good looks, and his star-and-triangle tattoo.

"Go talk to Metro," I told Meg in a bitter monotone. "He looks alone."

Meg's confusion was evident in her green eyes. She had reason to fear what she saw in mine. I marched toward Meza.

"I want to talk to you," I said.

He wouldn't look at me. Instead, he continued to study the wire sculpture, speaking softly in Spanish to the woman in cream-and-butter silks.

I could feel the punch coming in the balls of my feet. I was a second, maybe less, from giving his mouth my best shot.

"Outside," Meza said suddenly, his composure intact. Together, we walked to the door, Metro following a few steps behind.

"And tell your creature I have a gun," I said.

Meg stared from the back of the room. Meza stepped outside and Bodyguard snapped to. I followed close on Meza's heels. My hand inside my jacket, I held the cold .38 that Bodyguard had sold to me the night before. I'd kill them both if they wanted me to.

Nineteen

"Keep the bookie inside," Meza commanded of Bodyguard. "I can handle this."

The biker slowed his step as he walked away from the gallery windows, toward the corner. I stayed behind him, forcing Meza to throw his words over his shoulder as he walked.

"That gun don't mean shit to me," he spat.

My anger had swelled into a thickness I could chew.

"What's it, Rooster? Huh, what's it tonight?" he asked when we finally faced each other. "You get all hot and bothered about some broad and you want to mess with me."

"You know who broke Danny Harrison's hands."

"That's all, Mr. Killer?" Meza settled in. "Look, Rooster, I know. They screwed up bad. Your friend Danny is well known to me." He paused to see if he should go on. "He's in with the cops in KCK. As good as one of them. The cops will ride these guys into jail on little things now, anything they can dream up. Yeah, they screwed up bad, Rooster. But not me. Not me."

"I want to know who paid them."

"You going to shoot me? You that stupid?"

"I want to know who paid them," I said without a trace of emotion in my voice. My body was so tense it hummed.

"You aren't stupid, Rooster. You're just mad because you don't understand what's going down in your neighborhood. You want to know who paid them, but you already know. You want somebody to say it for you."

"Tell me what I already know."

"Why should I? Why should I talk to a man with blinders on?" Meza stepped by me, heading back to the gallery.

I'd made up my mind to follow him, to catch Meza at the door and press the pistol against his back, when Meza stopped in his tracks.

"Dammit," he said, throwing his hands down to his side in the edge of the streetlight glow. "You tell Ray Junior nobody pushes Meza, okay? You tell him what I'm telling you right now, Rooster. You say it out loud, and maybe you'll hear it for yourself."

Meza stepped closer, into the glow.

"It was a woman," he said, speaking each word carefully, separately, a teacher working after school with a problem pupil, a coach explaining a fundamental rule of the game. "It was her stuff you stole and she wanted it back. And you know what, Rooster?"

The green Ford showed up. It had turned onto State Line from Forty-seventh, crawling north.

"You're the one who didn't do anything about it," Meza charged. "I told Ray Junior that someone tried to hire me. He told you, Rooster. He told you, Rooster, and you didn't do shit. You sat there on your ass while they busted up Danny's hands. You knew who it was all—"

That's when Meza took a bullet in the butt. Without saying a word or crying out, he folded to the sidewalk and I was right on top of him. An automatic pistol of some kind buried lead into the brick wall above our heads. The car was moving or we'd have been dead. A four-door Crown Victoria.

I rolled over in time to see a brick crash through the Ford's windshield on the driver's side. It braked to a sudden stop, one tire up on the curb, its headlights turned out. Bodyguard was right behind the brick, high-stepping it across the street, leaping onto the hood of the Ford with a resounding crash and rolling over and off before the noise died down.

Bodyguard had the driver's door wrenched open and the assailant pulled out onto the sidewalk, scrambling for recovery.

"You don't mess with Meza!" Bodyguard shouted repeatedly as he mercilessly beat the small man, who'd lost his gun.

Meza's blood pooled on the sidewalk. People were coming out of the gallery now.

"You okay?" I asked my horizontal companion.

"Who is it?" he asked, pushing the words through clenched teeth. "Who is that?"

"What I want to know is where Bodyguard got that brick." Maybe he pulled it out of the wall with his teeth.

"He carries it with him," Meza said calmly. "You want to call an ambulance for me, or what."

Waiting was the worst part. A young man in a baseball jacket came by the booth Metro and I shared at Jack's, said something to the Creole bookie.

"Tomorrow," Metro said, pouring fresh beers. "I never handle money when I'm drinking. What was the score?"

"Eight to three," the intruder informed us. "Bo had four ribbies." Then he was gone.

"The Royals won," I said, trying to gloat and not quite managing it.

"Yeah, maybe you're on a roll."

It wouldn't be long, I thought, until Warman came looking for me. And I wouldn't be hard to find.

"Why is it," Metro was asking, "we sit around these bars every night?"

"What do you mean *we*, dickhead?"

"Besides business, Rooster. I've given it a lot of thought while you were in Seattle. The After Hours Club . . ." Metro shook his head as if the story were a sad one. "Everybody wants to be in love."

I waited for clarification.

"That's it?" I finally asked. "Everybody wants to be in love?"

"Yeah. When we're not in love, we hang out here with the other characters. Somebody falls in love, they're out. They might come around for a drink now and then, but they don't hang out, you know what I mean. They don't stick around till the bar closes and that's what *after hours* means, isn't it?"

"You're pining, Metro."

"Sure I am. But it's my job to be here. This is where I work. I've watched all of us for four or five years now, doing my sports book. And that's what we all do. We fall in love, we're at Worlds of Fun riding the roller coaster. Break up or have a problem and we're right back here with the group, shooting the shit."

"It's not the beer?"

"It's family, Rooster. Close as it gets. There's no place else to go when there's no place to go. Hell, we're adults, man. We're going bald. We see our kids every other weekend, if that. You get Rosalinda back and I'll be seeing you maybe once, maybe twice a month. Come Christmas.

"You look at these other couples hugging it up, their whole lives wrapped around each other. And we say, 'They got theirs,' and 'We're after ours.' That's the After Hours Club, Rooster. You know that I want you to get yours, I really do, but . . ."

"I'm not giving up, Metro. I've been through worse."

"No, you haven't," he said. "You looked in a mirror

lately? You look like shit. And you're so tired you're slurring your words."

"I'm slurring my words?"

"Yeah, dammit, it scares me. Your speech is all screwed up and your mouth looks like it's going to fall off, man, and you haven't had that much to drink. I know you, Rooster."

"I'm just tired, Metro. You said it yourself."

"Maybe. Maybe you ain't tired enough."

I stretched out on my back in the motel room, on the bed where Rosalinda and I had made love. I cried till I choked and couldn't stop choking. I had to sit up. I had the gun in one hand, waiting for something, for anything to happen. Waiting, I believed then, was the worst part. It was just the same old lonely crap.

I'd thought about what Rick Meza had said. He was wrong about that. It hadn't been Rosalinda's things I'd stolen from Inside Moves. It had been Warman's.

I don't know what the biker had told them at the hospital, but nobody knocked on the door. Metro and I had left the gallery before the cops came. Right now, parked outside were an unmarked Dodge, and a fancy blue Cadillac that had looked empty when I returned to the room after dropping Metro off at his car.

In Kansas City you recognize the people you know and don't know by their cars. I wondered what kind of car Marc Morelli drove these days. Not a blue Cadillac, I was sure. I wondered what Rosalinda wore to bed with Joe Warman.

The ringing of the phone hours later tumbled me from a sleep stupor. There was a tickle at the back of my throat I couldn't swallow. It was nearly six A.M. as I picked up the phone in the dimly lit motel room. Just one more way to start a Thursday.

"Alton?" the voice said.

It was Rosalinda.

My pulse leapt, my dulled brains stung at the sound of her voice.

"Yes," I said, clearing my throat with some difficulty. "I thought you'd call." *Prayed* is more like it.

"Oh, Alton," she said weakly. "I need you."

"What's the matter?" I asked, instantly alert. Warman hadn't put her up to this. But he'd done something.

"Everything, darling. Absolutely everything," she sobbed. "Can you come now? I need you, Alton."

"I'll be right there," I vowed.

"Please," Rosalinda said. "Please hurry."

She hung up. I stood in place, teetering, the phone to my ear, trying to quiet the deafening pace of my heartbeat. "I hope you got all that," I said into the receiver for the benefit of the wiretap. I slammed down the phone.

I flung on my jacket, put on my shoes. The Dodge was gone from outside. The blue Cadillac was also missing. Must be eating breakfast, I thought, quick-stepping it into the crisp morning.

Pulling into the Saturday morning traffic on Rainbow, I played back in my mind everything Rosalinda had just said. I could hear the tremor of her voice as if I were hearing her speak the words for the first time. She needed me. Rosalinda, the woman who cared about things other than price tags and profits, was back. I turned her voice on again, as you would turn on a radio, and basked in the sound of it driving me toward her.

I made love to her from fewer and fewer and fewer streets away, racing down Ward Parkway in the tan Camaro. Warman's Mercedes convertible was parked around the rear of the house. I pulled in behind it.

Rosalinda needed me. I pictured her tied to the bed, helpless, her phone call overheard. I saw Warman's gun being placed to her head. I saw blood matting her almond hair. Her blue eyes clouded. Then closed.

The back door was unlocked. Stepping inside, I heard

music playing. I followed the sound up the stairs. Grimacing with the pain in my knee, I ran, hopped, skipped, and jumped along the carpeted hall to a closed bedroom door. Inside, the radio blared.

My gun out and ready for anything, I pushed open the door. I spun in place inside the room. The bed was mussed. But no one was there. I stared at the radio alarm clock for a moment, then rushed out of the room.

She had to be somewhere. I found my way back downstairs. Sirens wailed along Ward Parkway, growing louder as they approached the house. My entry must have set off the silent alarm. Rosalinda was somewhere in the house, somewhere hidden, waiting to be rescued. Warman could be behind any door, waiting to spring.

I found him in the next room, sitting in a high-back leather chair. The telephone was ringing. Two walls of the study were lined from ceiling to floor with bookshelves. Antique marionettes, sporting lurid smiles, outnumbered the books on the oak shelves. Red lights flashed across the narrow Venetian blinds.

"Rosalinda!" I yelled. "Rosalinda!"

An upper wedge of Warman's head was missing. A .32-caliber automatic rested between his slack legs, covered by a blood-smeared hand. It looked like a suicide the grotesque puppets had borne witness to. Puppets with doll eyes.

Was she dead, too? Someone had turned off the answering machine. The phone finally stopped ringing. Warman may have killed her before killing himself. In fact, it was damned likely. I moved from room to room in a daze.

Halfway up the stairs, to check the bedroom again, to look under it, an excited voice asked that I freeze. The cops were here. One was in the room. But where was Rosalinda? Tranced, still walking, I mumbled to myself, "You're too late, you're too late." The police thought I was referring to them.

The officer tersely requested that I let go of the gun.

Twenty

The dark blue Cadillac idled at the curb outside the municipal building downtown.

I told them everything. None of it pleased Lieutenant Felker, whose Metropolitan Squad surveillance team verified that I'd been in my motel room until at least five-forty A.M., when they'd left to grab a quick breakfast and gas the Dodge. Felker offered no information and no theories. He took my statement and released me. The police were busy looking for Rosalinda, tracking down the itinerary Warman had given to Felker.

To keep from being held pending charges of a federal offense, I failed to surrender the cassette of Warman talking to the arsonist. First, I needed to know if Rosalinda were alive, then I'd stick the thing in the mail.

The Cadillac's horn sounded as I limped down the multitude of concrete steps toward the street, my left knee biting with each movement. Once I hit bottom, the driver's window whirred down on its electric motor. "Hop in," Ray Sargent, Sr., said.

"They catch you with a gun?" he asked, his eyes of experience boring into mine over our coffee cups at the International House of Pancakes on Broadway. I'd just finished an omelette and a short stack, having explained Ray, Jr.'s role in everything along with my own theory that the videotape of Rosalinda, Beth, and Kathleen wasn't the motive for any of this. Sargent had tended to agree.

"I said I found it on the kitchen table at Warman's house. When I found the body, I went back and picked it up for self-defense."

"Warman's not going to argue the point," Sargent said, his voice a music of youthful strength making its way over the gravel of a riverbed, over and through the stones of age.

"You know where she is, Rooster. Did you tell Felker?"

"What do you mean?"

Sargent chuckled. "Ruddick works for me, Rooster. I had him feed the tape back to you after he pulled the tap from Warman's phone." The light caught the silver handcuffs pin in the older man's lapel. It winked at me.

"And Warman?"

"I didn't trust him," Sargent confessed. "You know, Rooster, you only have to be a whore once to know it isn't worth the terrible bother. Money buys my professional expertise. It doesn't buy my loyalty."

"You gave him the tape of my call last night, didn't you?"

"Of course I did."

"And you knew I was playing with him?"

"Perhaps I suspected that. He paid me to tap your phone, not to interpret the messages. Like I said." Sargent shrugged it off. "Besides, it worked, didn't it? That's what you wanted."

"I wanted something to happen. I didn't mean for . . ."

"So is there anything to this stamp thing?"

"I'm afraid so," I answered. "It's big money, real big money. The Kelly girl found out about it and tried to move in."

"You still think it was him, don't you?" Sargent asked,

puzzled. The private detective was shaking his silver head. There was no hope for me was the message. "Here's something Felker might not have told you," he went on. "Warman was left-handed."

"The gun was in his left hand," I said. "It was in his left hand in his lap."

"The bullet entered the right side of his head. He didn't kill himself. Someone else did, and she set you up with that phone call."

"That's your opinion. There may be people you don't know about."

"I listened to the call, Rooster, remember? She said exactly what you wanted to hear. What any man would want to hear. Open your eyes. She wasn't calling you from the house. She was at the airport or, hell, she was already out of town. He'd been dead a few hours, that's why Felker let you out."

"Anything's possible," I said, irritated.

"You think it's her brother, Rooster? He's been accounted for. Madder than hell, but accounted for. Seems a motorcycle gang visited him late last night, tore up his place, locked him in the trunk of his car. Took Polaroids of him with their dicks in his mouth and a gun to his head. Left them lying around."

"It's not her," I said for the last time.

"I've been involved in these things for what seems like forever," Sargent growled. "I remember following you around after that botched bank job."

"It wasn't botched," I said.

"I remember *her*, Rooster." He tapped his brow with his forefinger. "My kid and you did okay, you came up with some things the police would have missed altogether. But you're missing something they've got."

"If you say impartiality, I'll hit you in the mouth."

"The autopsy, Rooster. They have the autopsy."

"For your information, I got that," I sputtered. "I've got

that and I've got a history with Rosalinda. I know her better than you or the cops or Joe Warman ever could."

"If you got the autopsy, you *forgot* the autopsy," Sargent said calmly. "There was a woman in bed with Kathleen Kelly the night she was killed. Now, who do you think it was? It wasn't the little girl my son's taking care of, you already know that. Felker already knows that."

There was nothing to say. My knee hurt like hell from sitting so long. Sargent drank from his coffee, his gold watch glinting in the sunlight that came through the window. A housefly buzzed against the pane, trapped not by glass, but by its own attraction to the light outdoors.

"Go ask her yourself," Sargent suggested. "You don't think Felker's going to make the drive, do you? So go ask her yourself if you can't use your own head to figure it out. What is it, five or six hours from here?"

She could be dead. There'd been a handful of things to do before leaving Kansas City. I'd even found time to drive by our missing house on Fairmount Street after Ray Sargent, Sr., dropped me off at my car. I believed I caught a glimpse of the small two-story Victorian as it had once stood.

There was plenty to think about on the drive to St. Louis. I sipped from a pint of Johnnie Walker Red, having brought along a friend. Johnnie Walker and missing women never talk back; they only burn. One of the things I did before leaving was buy another gun. I didn't tell Johnnie Walker about that. I didn't say a word.

It wasn't loaded. Under normal circumstances, I might have been. I was in a spiral of descent that felt very much like flying, as falling great distances must feel until you hit the ground. Eventually, I maneuvered the rented Camaro into the underground parking lot of the Chase Park Plaza Hotel.

Something big ached. Something big was already dead,

but something even bigger was being kept alive. I loved the woman.

I'd come to touch something, to revel in it, to ignite the cinders in Rosalinda before there was no more oxygen to feed the flame. I'd brought the gun to hold still the target of my love should she mistakenly decide to run.

I rode the elevator directly to her floor. Hurrying along corridors connecting the newer sections of the hotel with the old, I found her room number, found her door. I didn't knock. I didn't wait. I stood back on my left leg, my bad knee, and kicked ferociously out with my good one.

My left knee wrenched and almost gave out. Yet, the wood molding had splintered. I kicked once more and fell with the effort, fell in blinding pain.

The knee popped free of the tendons, slid sideways, popped, as the door rocked, gave way. My left leg collapsed under me. I was unable to walk. I cursed both the sharpness and the depth of the pain, writhing on the carpet in the hall. Cradling my leg, I managed to crawl into the room, tears filling my eyes. I swung the door closed. It banged against the damaged frame and stayed there.

I sat with my back against the bed, fighting to breathe, carefully stretching out my leg. The room was dark and empty. I drew up my knee, thankful it still worked, and nearly screamed.

Able to see well enough to make out the details of the room as I rocked my knee, I gritted my teeth and cried. Thank God this wasn't on television. You couldn't pay me enough to play football.

In a few minutes, I'd mustered the courage to stand. If I took it easy, very easy, the kneecap would stay where it belonged. I had to walk carefully, making sure I didn't twist my leg to either side as I stepped gingerly upon it. Her bags were on the bed, unpacked. She'd brought two suitcases.

Rosalinda had taken her purse, but something just as interesting caught my eye. The top of Rosalinda's smaller suitcase was latched shut by a combination lock. Instead of fooling with that, I freed the cloth-and-cardboard hinge of the case's top. Inside was a leather portfolio not much larger than a schoolgirl's notebook.

I limped to the Robo-bar and removed an airline-size bottle of Scotch. I twisted off the small cap, gulped the burning liquor, and grabbed another. I waited for my hands to stop shaking. Taking fragile baby steps, massaging my knee with one hand, I made it to the elevator, rode it to the lobby, and hobbled to the hotel bar. Though painfully, my knee began to accept the weight of my body.

I stood in the entryway, waiting for my vision to adjust to the darkness of the room. The waitresses were dressed as jockeys, wearing black net hose instead of baggy white pants. There were pictures of horses, some I recognized, on the walls, along with an occasional saddle with irons and other pieces of tack.

I surveyed the occupants of the large room and wasn't surprised to see her.

She sat at a table with her back to me, but there was no mistaking Rosalinda. I could have smelled her there. I stepped around the approaching hostess, who carried a padded menu larger than the portfolio tucked under my arm.

"I'm meeting friends," I said from the side of my mouth, and guardedly walked toward Rosalinda and her companion, an older man who smiled around large teeth as the two of them talked.

Rosalinda wore a formal black, scoop-necked dress with a string of gleaming pearls. Conservative, but fitting, I thought, for the business she was there to conduct. A white beaded clutch purse lay on the table beside her glass of red wine. Each earring was a trace of gold encircling a small, perfect pearl.

"May I?" I asked, pulling back a chair and resting my weight on it.

The older man, whose skin was the particular shade of

gray associated with cadavers, looked first at me, then back to Rosalinda, questioning her with the expression on his face.

"This is Mr. Kovel," Rosalinda began in a severe tone.

"He's leaving," I barked, sitting cautiously on the side of the chair. "In fact, he's leaving right now."

I looked only at Rosalinda. Her agitation showed merely as a slight twitch at the corner of her intolerant smile. "Tell him, lover, that I've got a gun," I added. Rosalinda was as beautiful as ever. Gorgeous.

She gestured with her hand and a small, practiced toss of her hair for the man to leave. He needed little prodding. As he rose from the table, the waitress done up like Willie Shoemaker approached. "Would you care for a cocktail, sir?" she asked of my shoulder.

"Nothing," I said, still staring at Rosalinda. "I'm finishing his."

This was the hard part. The rate of her breathing increased as Rosalinda eyed the portfolio tucked snuggly under my arm. I handed it to her and waited.

She snatched it from my hand and frantically worked open the zipper. Inside were three previously folded photocopies of the sheets of invert error stamps. I picked up her purse in my left hand. Though small, it was large enough and heavy enough to be holding a gun.

Rosalinda's eyes flashed. "You bastard," she hissed.

It wasn't the words that hurt me. I deserved as much. It was her eyes. Her so-often-dreamed-of eyes. They held nothing but livid hate for me.

"How much were you getting?" I asked casually, ignoring the new pain that pressed in on my chest to choke the life from me. Through the stunning heartache, I forced my hand over hers and squeezed it. I wanted to get some answers before I told her where the stamps were.

Her reaction to my touch was to draw back. But I could feel Rosalinda struggling within herself. She smiled bravely, turned her hand over inside mine so that our palms touched, our heartbeats.

"It's not too late, Alton. We could . . . you and I . . ." She wrapped her fingers up over the edge of my palm. "He won't leave. He just went back to his room. We could bring him the stamps later tonight."

Someone at the bar was watching us.

"How much?" I repeated.

"Millions," Rosalinda promised, a chill to her voice. "Where are they, darling? What have you done with them? Oh, Alton, I knew you'd find me if anyone could. I knew you were coming."

"I'm here," I said blankly.

Rosalinda's thoughts painted her face. She was remembering, her lips moving in silence. She smiled momentarily, then whispered, "She almost ruined everything, that little bitch. She deserved it, Alton. Nothing else would have worked."

I waited to be convinced. Killing Kathleen Kelly couldn't have been the only alternative. I pressed my hand down on Rosalinda's. I was nearly moved to hold her. Instead, I looked away from her.

"You had the stamps all along," I said, releasing the pressure on her hand, but not on her life.

"Yes, of course," she said, her voice once again that of a coconspirator. "A CIA manager, he really must remain nameless, coerced a postmaster where the original pane of a hundred had been sold into handing over the remaining sheets. Word of the stamps began to leak and he got nervous, Alton. He called Joe. You see, darling, Joe had a reputation for dealing upscale collectibles. He came up with a hundred and twenty thousand dollars, a paltry sum, really."

There was a lilt to Rosalinda's voice. She was telling the most exciting thing that had ever happened to her as if the story were one I'd enjoy hearing. She'd referred to Warman in the past tense. It was clear to me she'd killed him, too. What wasn't clear was whether or not she was completely insane with greed.

"The manager turned it over to the covert-action fund, most of it anyway. Everyone was happy with the deal. They never dreamed the stamps were worth this much. Only you and I know, darling. You and I."

"Until the story broke months later, when the stamps from the original hundred began to show up on the market," I said. "Everyone knows what they're worth."

"It's what we'd been waiting for," Rosalinda said, squeezing my hand too tightly, holding on to her own emotional roller coaster ride. "The CIA wanted them back, of course. We told them a Saudi had purchased them as a long-term investment, that the stamps wouldn't surface for years."

"Then you had to sell the stamps without the CIA catching on." I played along. "Tricky, but it could be done."

"It can still be done, Alton. Joe wanted to wait for the publicity to drive the prices up. And he was so right, darling. We're talking about millions of dollars, you and I. Millions of dollars tonight." Rosalinda was breathless, her palm sweaty.

"Millions," I repeated.

"Right here in the hotel. He brought the money with him, Alton. He'll bring it to my room, if we ask him to. You can make certain everything goes all right."

I wished. "Who killed Marty Ryan?" I asked.

Rosalinda's blue eyes shifted, the question taking her by surprise. It seemed so irrelevant.

"You killed him," I said for her, wanting her to argue, to lie.

"Yes," Rosalinda said. "He was a pro. He'd never have let Joe get that close. With me, his guard was down." I knew the feeling. The love of my life had shot a man in the head as a cold-blooded act of commerce.

"Who killed Kathleen?" I pressed her hand until it hurt.

Rosalinda glanced away, then back again. There were dollar signs where her eyes had been.

"We had to," she said. "She couldn't be trusted, Alton. And she was demanding half, *half* of everything. It was her own fault."

"Who pulled the trigger?"

"Does it matter?" Rosalinda attempted to pull her hand out from under mine. She avoided the answer when she should have lied. Now, it was too late to lie.

"To me it does," I said. "It matters very much."

Rosalinda killed her. If it had been Warman, Rosalinda would have said so immediately. Rosalinda tied her up, had sex with her, and shot her. Taking care of business.

"And your husband, I suppose it was his own fault, too. He wanted half. Was that it, Rosalinda?"

My face darkened. I wasn't prepared for the anger that overtook me and I was nearly shouting.

"No," she said coolly. "He wanted to control it all, and me. He was treating me like . . . like a wife."

It was a mistake I'd never make. I thought I'd resolved everything on the drive from Kansas City, but a large part of me was still dancing a tightrope over fire. I was still in love with her. And she had killed them all.

Her motive had been greed. Rosalinda had gone flipping fucking mad. What kept me from slapping her was that our reunion had only just begun. The night was young and I planned to return to Rosalinda's hotel room with her and see what would happen there.

Twenty-One

"Shall we?"

Rosalinda scooped up the portfolio, while I held on to her purse. I told her I'd had an accident with my leg and that we'd need to walk slowly, arm in arm, side by side. I also reminded her I was carrying a gun. There was nothing to say in the elevator, but Rosalinda kept talking.

The two of us, she said, could get away from all this, the rest of the world. We could create our own universe to rule. Anywhere we wanted. For as long as we lived.

That was the question.

I wanted to stretch her money-grubbing claws across the leg of a toppled chair and stamp them into bloody pieces. As my own heart had been.

Rosalinda had made love to me. Had it been a ruse to keep me occupied while Ryan torched the house on Fairmount Street? The narrow, disappearing bruises on the inside of her wrists were the brands of her changed existence. They were the marks of a suicide, after all. Rosalinda had killed the woman I loved.

She pushed ahead of me into her room, ignoring the damaged door frame. Finding the switch, she turned on the lights. Then, tossing the portfolio on the bed, Rosalinda scurried about the room, looking like a child on an Easter egg hunt.

"Where are they, Alton, where are they?" She could have smelled the stamps if she tried.

"In the lavatory," I said, watching her, unamused. "In the sink."

"You didn't get them wet, did you?" she blathered, rushing into the bathroom. I hobbled behind, removing the gun from inside my jacket, inside my belt, letting her beaded purse fall to the carpet.

Rosalinda turned on the bathroom light, simultaneously turning on the overhead ventilation fan. It whirred, sucking the breath out of her lungs, lifting it toward the ceiling, an invisible cloud of internal ruin. The color drained from her fine face.

"You son of a bitch!" she screamed. Rosalinda stared at me, as if frozen in horror. A corner of her upper lip curled involuntarily, revealing her teeth. I could make out only small remnants of the Rosalinda left behind in her twisted features, her twisted mind.

The lavatory sink held the ashes of her precious stamps. The burned sheets of stamps could have been blown into a powder of ashes by no more breath than it takes to blow a kiss. Seeing the burned stamps had destroyed the new Rosalinda as surely as she had destroyed the Rosalinda I loved. I wondered what was left.

Something inside of me, propped up by a trick knee, longed to comfort her. I removed my left hand from my jacket pocket and held out to Rosalinda her loop-and-pendant earring, the shiny relic of our past.

Rosalinda gathered strength. A dab of foaming saliva dried in the corner of her mouth. She drew herself up for one more outburst and, staring at me from wide red eyes, from the eyes of an animal, I thought, lunged forward and hit me in the face with all her wild strength channeled into a single, savage blow.

It hurt.

It put out the fire and it hurt.

The bushfire of my raging love was reduced to an irritating cinder in the eye, a bruise, a drop of blood where my tooth had cut my lip. With one slap of her hand, she felled me. The knee gave way easily, painfully, and I collapsed backwards, dropping the gun as she pounced upon me.

Rosalinda snatched up the heavy .38 and stepped back. I opened my eyes from a squint to see her actually pulling the trigger, a grin on her face, a terrible grin of irretrievable madness. The gun was empty. I'd have let her run if it had come to my using the damn thing.

Lieutenant Felker, who'd ridden to St. Louis with me, who'd let me drive and drink, who'd followed us to the room from his seat downstairs in the bar, saw things differently. He'd come to take her into custody. He'd come into her hotel room through the broken door, delayed by the second elevator. I didn't even hear the shots the police detective fired into Rosalinda's chest from just outside the bathroom door.

But I watched what they did to her, propelling Rosalinda slightly backwards, away from me, pushing her against the wall. I watched what they did to her and what they did to me. She died with her eyes open. I believe she is seeing me still.

Maybe it had been a mirror all along, my future with Rosalinda, a mirror reflecting the past, a mirror that had slipped from my grasp. A mirror in pieces, catching shards of empty sunlight and turning them back. It isn't my fault that

Randy Russell

I'm still in love with her. That I find among the pieces something of value.

Speaking of value, I saved a block of the invert error stamps. I tore four from one of the sheets before burning them in the bathroom sink. If you're interested, leave word for me at Jack's.